Scarred with Fortune

Scarred with Fortune

Anne Coltman

Library of Congress Control Number:		2011918975
ISBN:	Hardcover	978-1-4653-8570-3
	Softcover	978-1-4653-8569-7
	Ebook	978-1-4653-8571-0

To order additional copies of this book, contact:
Xlibris Corporation
1-888-795-4274
www.Xlibris.com
Orders@Xlibris.com
104565

Table of Contents

Faith is the torch that lights our paths
It sustains us in times of adversity
Nourishes our belief in life and humanity
Strengthens our will to succeed
And revives that spirit which keeps us forging ahead.

—Anne Coltman

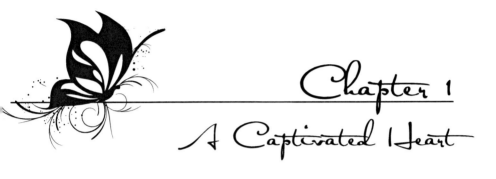

Chapter 1
A Captivated Heart

It was a sunny afternoon in early August the summer of 1958. Fiona stood at the window of their newly painted two-storied Victorian house where she lived with her parents, John and Elsie Leighton, and her brother Gerald. Her eyes focused down Sunny Lane, hoping to get a glimpse of her heartthrob, Stephen Brimm, when he sped down the road past her house as he so often did in his dad's Chevy. She had just finished drying her hair and had her dress and shoes all laid out for his going-away party that evening. The two teenagers attended high school together and graduated with the class of '58. Although Steve was being sent away to attend his father's alma mater, Fiona was going to a local college. This was the first time she was invited to a party by a boy. All her girlfriends were invited as well—in fact, the whole class was invited—and that was why Fiona was allowed to attend. Having conservative parents made it difficult for her to have a boyfriend or see Steve other than at school, so she was particularly happy that she could avail this opportunity of being with him.

The evening could not come quickly enough for Fiona. Two of her friends stopped by to accompany her to the party. Her father offered to give the young ladies a ride and saved them the walk to the Brimm's residence. She promised not to be home too late and waved at him as he turned the car around and headed home.

The girls had an enjoyable time, especially Fiona who returned home feeling starry-eyed and giddy and went to bed in her pretty lace dress. The next week, Steve left for college. Before he did, he sent Fiona a note telling her that he was thinking of her and promised to be back home for Thanksgiving. He assured that he would write her every week and made her promise to do the same. She hid the note where no one else could find it and read it every day. It was the only thing that she had to hold on to that brought her close to him. She did not even get to see him after the night of the party. He just sent the note, and that was all she had. Fiona felt lost and empty but consoled herself that summer would soon be over and she would get to see Steve again somehow. She tried to concentrate on the new classes she had signed up for and took up reading as a hobby to keep her mind occupied. She visited the local library regularly with her brother and volunteered to help with "children's story hour" during the remaining summer holidays. She was happy when college reopened and immersed herself in her studies.

In the middle of the first semester, Fiona found it difficult to get out of bed in the mornings. She began to get worried about her increasing tiredness and loss of appetite. She never skipped morning breakfast before but started to do so quite regularly as it became difficult for her to keep any of it down. Unable to concentrate on her studies, Fiona decided to quit college after one week of disguising her feelings at the breakfast table and having a hard time staying awake in class. She did so without her parents' knowledge. The first few days, she pretended to have a sore throat; but when morning sickness prevailed and her mother took her to a doctor, her pregnancy was confirmed. Having received a letter from Steve telling her about his college, Fiona replied immediately, letting him know of her dilemma.

The Leightons were both very angry and disappointed in their only daughter. John Leighton refused to speak to her when she refrained from telling them whom she was with. Elsie preached to her every day but to no avail. Fiona kept sending letters to Steve but got only one reply. She decided to wait until he came home for Thanksgiving. She felt sure she would have a chance to speak to him then. However, he made excuses to his parents, saying he had urgent papers to finish for upcoming exams, and would not make it home for the holiday. This was not the truth. Steve had no intentions of going back to Hillcrest since he was unsure of what to expect from Fiona or her parents and did not wish his parents to have any knowledge of the situation. His final letter of rejection, along with the fact that he did not come home for Thanksgiving, made Fiona sink deep into depression. She was now, more than ever, determined not to tell her parents who the father of her baby was. Even though her mother had suspected it might be Steve Brimm, she kept her thoughts to herself. She remembered how thrilled Fiona was to attend his going-away party and thought it odd that he only wrote her one letter and never called on her during the holiday. Nevertheless, she refrained from mentioning it as she realized how precarious a situation it would be if her husband, John, found out. She knew he would confront Steve's parents and cause further embarrassment. This made her very angry, and she treated her daughter with utter contempt.

Fiona felt disgraced and alone. She could not face her parents and was scared of the thought of having to abide by the consequences of her actions. When her sickness finally subsided a few months later, she was able to think about the future. She pulled herself together and decided to get through it and get back to her studies. She isolated herself from friends, family members, and her parents and came out of her bedroom only to get food when everyone else was asleep at night or when no one was home during the day. She slipped into the bathroom when she was sure no one would see her because it was situated right next to her room. She became her own prisoner.

The family was detached and unhappy and could not capture the spirit of the Christmas season, which came very quickly. Elsie was anxious to have her daughter emerge from isolation for the holidays, but Fiona could not cease being depressed; her gratuitous tears washed her face each night. She somehow found the courage to tear herself away from her room and eat breakfast and dinner with the family on Christmas Day. John Leighton did not let his anger and disappointment overcome him then; it was the first time he spoke to his daughter in several weeks. Gerald was glad to see his sister again and tried not to look surprised at her drawn features.

Stephen Brimm returned home for Christmas but kept to himself and his family. He stayed away from Sunny Lane and made no contact with Fiona, although she thought a lot about him and his family during those miserable days. She knew how influential his father was and became afraid of the knowledge that he could take away the baby from her once he knew of his grandchild.

A very cold winter ushered in the New Year and found Fiona isolated again in her room. The days grew long and dreary. No one kept an account of the weeks that had gone by, not even Fiona. She placed herself in her own winter wonderland and was not even aware that spring was upon them. On May 8, her water broke, and she was quickly taken to the local hospital where she gave birth to a son after several hours of labor and normal delivery. Her parents were relieved that she was all right. They had mixed feelings about their grandson but decided to put them aside.

After taking her home, John Leighton surprised his daughter with a crib and a carriage for the baby. Elsie took care of her grandson and her daughter for the first couple of weeks until Fiona felt confident to take care of the tiny baby by herself. She reconciled with her dad and made up for all the hurt by being as loving and kind to him as she did before she became pregnant. When the baby was six weeks old, Fiona took him for walks most afternoons on her trip to the pharmacy to pick up baby milk and the evening newspapers for her dad. Once she even had the courage to venture out of her way, pushing her carriage as she strolled along the street where Steve's parents lived. Realizing what she had done, she quickly hurried home and made a secret promise never to go near them again.

It was on one of her afternoon walks that she met Sandy McPherson while coming out of the store. He introduced himself and asked about her father, then admiring the baby, inquired if he was her little brother. Fiona was very shy; she smiled and quickly excused herself without answering him. He sensed her embarrassment as she walked away, so he made a few quick steps to catch up with her and asked her politely to give his regards to her father. She said she would, thanked him, and walked away once more. When she got home, Fiona never mentioned her encounter with Mr. McPherson to her father and forgot all about him after that day.

The next week, after stopping at the store to pick up the evening paper for her dad while on her usual walk with the baby, Fiona met Sandy again. After his first encounter with her, he made a habit of looking out for her in the afternoons. His office was at a real estate and tax agency situated right next to the pharmacy. From his desk, he had a full view of the street and could see when Fiona turned the corner and approached with her carriage. He started waiting for her to appear before leaving for the day; that way, he was certain to meet her outside the store.

Although she did not know him, Sandy McPherson knew Fiona since she was in high school and was attracted to her. He first saw her four years before when John Leighton stopped his car to speak to him briefly concerning his taxes. Fiona was in the car with her dad but paid no attention to the two men as they spoke. John Leighton had some paperwork for Sandy's boss who was attending to his taxes that year. The young man noticed the beautiful girl in the backseat, but she was oblivious of his presence since her eyes were focused on the magazine on her lap.

On that occasion, Sandy said hello, played briefly with the baby, and lingered outside the store until Fiona was out of sight. He made it a habit of showing up most days after that. One afternoon, three weeks after their first encounter, Fiona did some shopping at the store when she went to pick up the evening news for her dad. Besides baby supplies, she got cookies, bath soap for her mother, shaving cream for her dad, and a few bottles of soda. She placed the bags in the carriage with the baby and left the store. At that time, she did not see the young man who waited for her by the entrance of his office building. He walked up beside her, said hello, removed the bags from the carriage, and respectfully told her he would be happy if she allowed him to accompany her home. Fiona smiled and thanked him, and the two walked along without much conversation.

When she arrived home, Sandy helped her lift the carriage up a few steps and placed it on the patio. He rang the bell while she got the baby from the carriage, then greeted John Leighton as he opened the door. Handing him the bags, he explained that he was just helping Fiona with the load. After a short conversation about business, Sandy said good-bye to Mr. Leighton while Fiona disappeared into the house with the baby. John Leighton seemed fond of Sandy McPherson. He spoke of how kind and considerate the young man was, but his daughter merely shrugged, handed him the papers, kissed him on his forehead, and left the room in silence. She waited until her father retired in his armchair for the rest of the afternoon before slipping outside to bring in the carriage, which was left on the patio.

A few afternoons after that, Fiona met Sandy again. She was a bit friendlier to him and allowed him to escort her to her gate. After three months of casual meetings and light conversations while on the way home, Sandy decided to approach Mr. Leighton for his daughter's hand in marriage and did so without her knowledge. He already knew that the baby was her son although they never spoke about it. He was nervous about letting her know of his true feelings for her and preferred to speak to her father before doing so.

On that afternoon, Sandy waited for Fiona to enter the store, then left his office hurriedly to see her father before she returned home. He needed to have a few minutes alone with the elder gentleman. Fiona noticed that he was not waiting for her as he usually did when she was finished picking up the newspapers but thought nothing of it. She enjoyed slowly walking home, soaking up the cool fresh air as she pushed her carriage. Meanwhile, Sandy chatted a bit with John Leighton before getting around to telling him of his intention to marry his daughter. That proposal surprised John very much. He wondered why Sandy dropped in to see him since it had nothing to do with his taxes but did not expect to be asked for Fiona's hand in marriage. He sat with raised eyebrows, looking intently at the young man as he expressed his interest in Fiona and explained that he had admired her for a long time and was getting to know her better during the last three months. John did not seem suspicious about Sandy being the baby's father. As a matter of fact, he gave his consent after hearing Sandy acknowledge his desire to make Fiona happy and to be a father to the baby. John Leighton was curious to know if Sandy had discussed this with Fiona and felt somewhat satisfied to hear that he waited for his consent before doing so. John called Elsie to the room and asked her opinion of the young man. She expressed a bit of shock; unlike her husband, Elsie Leighton did not know Sandy McPherson at all. She thought it quite strange that this man should come out of nowhere and ask for their daughter's hand in marriage. Needless to say, she questioned him thoroughly. Sandy became nervous, but John was amused. He decided to intervene by telling his wife of their acquaintance and how long he knew the young chap.

In the midst of it all, Fiona returned home and was also surprised to find Sandy chatting with her parents. She said hello and left the room with the baby after handing her father the evening news. When Sandy stood up to leave, John Leighton called Fiona to accompany the young man to the door while he slumped into his armchair with the newspapers. At that moment, Elsie said good-bye to him and went back to fixing dinner. Fiona put the baby in his crib and went to the door as her dad requested. Then Sandy asked her to accompany him outside, but she hesitated, saying she had to attend to the baby.

"It will only take a minute," he said. "I have something important to discuss with you."

Fiona was curious. She stepped outside and closed the door. Sandy sat on a bench at the far end of the patio and requested Fiona to join him. He took her hand as she sat beside him and asked her if she would consider marrying him. He told her that he had already spoken to her parents about his feelings for her and hoped that she would consider his proposal. Fiona was confused and embarrassed. She stood up immediately, pulled her hand away from him, and reached for the door. Then saying good-bye, she closed it behind her, leaving Sandy alone in the patio feeling humiliated and rejected.

John and Elsie Leighton were very disappointed to learn that Fiona had refused Sandy's proposal. They were hoping that she would be interested in redeeming her dignity and did not even consider the fact that the man was just a casual acquaintance. They never asked her how she felt about Sandy McPherson. A sensation of entrapment overcame Fiona. It seemed that her parents were planning her life for her, and she secretly rebelled against it. Elsie became sad and distant from her daughter; John gave her the silent treatment once more. However, this time, Fiona refused to agonize over her parents' attitude and went about her daily chores, only having conversations with her brother Gerald since her parents had very little to say to her. Gerald adored his sister and was quite proud of his little nephew. He looked forward to him growing up so he could teach him to play the trumpet.

Fiona was not bothered that Sandy did not wait for her outside the store during the weeks that followed. She enjoyed her alone time, which allowed her to think about the outcome of her life as she sauntered down Sunny Lane. She contemplated being able to finish college and get a job, which would enable her to take care of herself and her son.

Steve never made it home for the summer holidays that year. He took an internship instead with a firm of engineers in the city where he attended college. He was, however, expected to return home for the coming Thanksgiving.

Chapter 2
The Expectation

The summer went by just as quickly as it came. Fiona knew that she would have to stop taking the baby out in the afternoons during the colder months. In fact, her mother told her so since the autumn afternoons were quite chilly. Nevertheless, on one of those afternoons, she decided to bundle him up and take him along with her as she went to the store to make her usual purchases. Sandy saw her approaching as he sat at his desk, gazing through the window of his office, but did not leave to meet her. She came out of the store with more bags than she could carry, so she picked up the baby, placed the bags in the carriage, and continued walking, carrying the child in one hand while pushing the carriage with the other. Sandy observed her predicament. The wind blew the shawl off the baby, and she stopped to fix it. As she let go of the carriage, it rolled away from her. Seeing this, he left the office and ran to stop the carriage. He removed the shopping bags and made Fiona put the baby back inside. He was pleasant, but she was her usual shy self. She thanked him and continued on her way home. He followed her silently. When she was close to home, Fiona apologized for their last meeting three weeks before. Sandy did not say much. He accepted her apology, placed the shopping bags on the patio, helped her lift the carriage to the front door, said good-bye, and left. No one noticed that he had helped her with the shopping; neither did she mention it. John and Elsie were looking at their favorite afternoon program and were both preoccupied when Fiona returned home.

A few days later, she returned to the store again. This time, she lingered inside for a while expecting to see Sandy McPherson, but he did not show up. She shopped on several occasions after that but made no contact with him. He always saw her from his window but had no desire to impose himself on her again.

Thanksgiving was two weeks away when Fiona stopped by the store earlier than usual one brisk sunny afternoon and decided to drop into the office to see Sandy. She was somewhat embarrassed at her audacity to do so. Also, he was just as surprised to see her and inquired if she needed help. She apologized for the intrusion and looked around the small storefront agency as she spoke, "Would you like to walk with me to the park when you are finished with work?"

Sandy was delighted and cautiously optimistic. "Maybe," he said, and they left the office together.

He bought a balloon for the baby, which he attached to the carriage, and they chatted casually as they walked around the park. Fiona expressed her apprehension at his proposal. "Let's call a truce, shall we?"

She felt awful for having hurt his feelings but made it quite clear that she did not want to be pitied. Sandy was a bit uncomfortable; he however mustered up enough courage to ask if she would give him a chance to prove his sincerity. She agreed, and they shook hands. Then he blew a kiss to the baby as they left the park.

Every day after that, Sandy met Fiona in front of the store holding the evening papers that he had already purchased for her. Then they strolled around the park chatting and getting better acquainted with each other. He sometimes pushed the carriage to allow her to gather up fresh falling leaves, something she loved to do as a little child. Everyone who saw them together during those days thought they were already a couple, and Sandy quickly realized that. He decided to try his luck by asking her again to marry him. He particularly wanted to do so before Thanksgiving, and since it was only three days away, he thought that was the best time and place. He tried to be more romantic about it this time since he realized that he acted too hastily before. He was stone-faced as he nervously spoke; he was not as confident as he would have liked to be. However, he managed to get the words out. Fiona smiled. She thought he looked silly because he seemed worried and afraid of being rejected in a public place. Instead of an answer, she questioned his intentions. His explanation made her blush. It gave her a good feeling about herself, but she got serious when he told her that he knew she was not in love with him at the moment and assured her that she would feel differently once they were together.

"You're assuming too much," she said arguably.

"Just give it some thought," he pleaded.

She reluctantly agreed. Then they left the park and made their way toward Sunny Lane. When Sandy stopped the carriage to make sure the baby was properly bundled up, Fiona invited him to come and visit the evening of Thanksgiving. She promised to let him know then how she felt about his friendship. He straightened up, shrugged in disbelief, then blew the baby a kiss and said good-bye. The young man watched as she turned the corner because she refused to allow him to accompany her home.

Fiona did not take the baby for his afternoon walk on the two days that followed. She spent the time helping her mother with preparations for Thanksgiving dinner. Elsie Leighton had casual and polite conversations with her daughter; nevertheless, she still revealed signs of disappointment in her. John pretty much kept to himself when Fiona was around. He rarely had anything much to say to her although he enjoyed playing with his grandson. He cared deeply for his daughter and couldn't help thinking that she let a good chance for happiness pass her by. However, the decision was purely Fiona's. Even though they were disappointed in her, they would never force her to do anything against her will.

Fiona woke up very early on the morning of Thanksgiving. She tidied her room, fed the baby, gave him a warm bath, dressed him, and took him to her parents' room. Having announced her presence with a knock on the door and a greeting, she hurriedly walked in and placed the child in her mother's arms, then said she was going to prepare breakfast. Gerald was delighted to help his sister in the kitchen. He was particularly happy to see her smile and tease him as she did when they were younger. After breakfast, he helped her with the dishes while their mother cleaned and decorated the dining table in preparation for Thanksgiving dinner. Fiona helped with the cooking and let her father and brother take care of the baby. She was very interested in the preparation of the meal and volunteered to make the pies. Her mother was a good cook, and Fiona was happy to learn from her. It seemed like old times again. However, Elsie was very cautious. Her daughter seemed a bit lighthearted, and she wondered if it had anything to do with the father of her child but refrained from asking.

The day went by smoothly. Violet, Elsie Leighton's older sister who had been widowed for several years, arrived in the early afternoon to visit the family and have dinner as she customarily did on Thanksgiving. Edgar and Alice Leighton, John's parents, accepted his invitation to Thanksgiving dinner as his turn for having them came around again. The old couple spent their Thanksgivings with a different family member each year. Now the time had come for them to be with their son John who was visibly anxious. Edgar and Alice had not seen Fiona's baby and knew very little about her pregnancy. John dreaded the questions concerning Fiona being a single mother and gave a lot of thought to how he would respond if his parents tried to make him feel responsible for the situation. He was more ashamed of not knowing who the father of his grandchild was than his daughter being an unwed mother.

He knew it would only be a matter of time before they engaged him in a serious conversation. So after they arrived, he kept busy helping add chairs to the table and making sure he had enough wine in the cooler. John avoided having those little business talks his dad looked forward to whenever they were together and was somewhat relieved that the old folks were so charmed with the baby that they didn't really notice that he had no time to sit and chat with them.

Just before everyone gathered, Elsie examined the dinner table to see if the place settings were all there. She noticed an extra chair without a place setting and inquired about it.

Fiona smiled. "Just in case we have a visitor," she said softly.

Elsie frowned. "Maybe we won't," she replied roughly, then pushed the chair aside before calling everyone to the table.

John's mother said a short and simple prayer of thanks as they stood around. When she was finished, they all sat and cheered John as he carved the turkey. Just as they were about to eat, the doorbell rang. Fiona jumped to answer it, hoping to get to the door before the bell sounded again. She did not want the ringing to wake the baby who slept in his carriage in the living room. She was anxious and felt a bit guilty as she opened the door. Sandy greeted her and gave her the pie he was carrying, then made his way into the house and approached John Leighton. He handed him a small burlap bag containing two bottles of fine wine and wished everyone a happy Thanksgiving.

The family looked quite surprised, but before anyone had a chance to speak, Fiona announced that she had invited Sandy to stop by. Elsie controlled her emotions, but John was visibly stunned. Fiona, sensing the tension, made the introductions, and Sandy exchanged greetings with everyone. Then she pulled up the chair her mother had removed earlier and fixed a place setting at the table. Sandy was then asked to join them for dinner, seated between Fiona and her father.

Grandpa Edgar passed a dish of yams to Sandy, saying, "Guest first. Now let's eat, shall we?"

Sandy helped himself and handed the dish to Fiona who sat on his right. They all laughed and talked during the meal, and an atmosphere of calm soon came over the room. As the conversation grew louder toward the end of the meal, the chatter woke the baby. Fiona heard his cries and rushed to get him. She returned and stood for a while between Sandy and her father with the baby in her arms. Her mother gave her a quizzical glance and was about to speak when Fiona blurted out, "I have something to say, Mom."

At that moment, everyone turned and looked at Fiona with some anticipation.

"I have accepted Sandy's proposal, and we would like to be married before Christmas if that is all right with you, Dad and Mom."

John Leighton looked a bit confused. His wife was shocked, but Gerald clapped his hands, and Aunt Violet shouted, "Congratulations!" while Papa and Mama Leighton, Fiona's grandparents, raised their glasses and smiled approvingly. Having overcome the initial shock, Elsie regained her composure and gave her daughter a gentle hug, something she had not done in several weeks. Her wide open eyes and raised eyebrows seemed to ask the question, "When did it all happen?" But she remained silent. Fiona rested her hand on the young man's shoulder, hoping he would make it easier for her. As her father replenished the wine glasses, Sandy seized the moment and stood up. He explained that he had been seeing Fiona for some time so they could get better acquainted and was hoping, when she got to know him better, she would agree to marry him. He confessed that he was still a bit unsure of her decision until her announcement.

"This has made me the happiest man alive," he confessed and promised John and Elsie that he would take good care of their daughter and grandson.

When he was finished, John held up his glass and exclaimed, "This calls for a celebration, bring in some more wine!"

After dinner, John took Sandy by the arm and led him into the living room where dessert and coffee would be served. He wanted to have a few minutes alone with the young man before everyone else gathered there. Fiona went up to her room to feed the baby while Aunt Violet and old Mama Leighton helped Elsie clean the table, do the dishes, and put away the leftovers. As the women were busy, Gerald took the chance to show his grandfather his new trumpet and baseball mitt that he got for his birthday. He loved spending time with his grandfather.

It seemed like a few hours had passed when the dinner bell rang again, signaling that dessert was being served in the living room. The family gathered, ate, and chatted while soft music played in the background. John had been so interested in talking with Sandy that he totally overlooked his daughter who felt somewhat rejected. Noticing her standing in the middle of the room, he silently beckoned her to sit next to him. In a whisper, John told his daughter how proud he was of her and how he admired her maturity. Then turning to Sandy, he asked the two young people when they would like to be married. Fiona spoke first. "The weekend before Christmas," she said firmly. Sandy agreed, saying that if that was convenient for the family, he would like to take his bride home for the holidays.

"Well, I think we should discuss plans for a very simple ceremony at home," John Leighton said.

"That would be fine with us," Sandy replied, nodding at Fiona as he spoke.

"Nothing big," she said. "Just a few cousins, uncles, and aunts."

Her father agreed and suggested they make arrangements with the town's registrar.

Chapter 3
Unconditional Love

In the weeks that followed, the Leighton household became a happy place once more. Elsie hugged her daughter frequently and took her shopping for a wedding dress and accessories. She also stopped by the local bakery to order a cake and pastries for the occasion. Uncles, aunts, and cousins were contacted and invited to a "small and simple" celebration for the couple. Sandy had the liquor store send over two cases of wine and a case of champagne. Aunt Violet agreed to make a few dishes, and Mama Leighton said she would spend some time with the family to help Elsie with preparations and cooking.

John Leighton was in favor of Sandy McPherson becoming his son-in-law. Sandy was a fine young man with good qualities and a gentle nature—who seemed more mature than his twenty-eight years—and most of all, loved Fiona unconditionally. When he was fourteen years old, Sandy lost his father to a railroad accident that left his mother partially paralyzed. She was fifty-seven years old at the time and had to make ends meet with a little help from relatives. Sandy took care of his mother in the years that followed. He started working fresh out of high school and was apprenticed to an accountant at the town's advertising agency. It was there that he met Alfred Gunning, the owner of Gunning's Real Estate and Tax Agency. After several years of helping Mr. Gunning with his ads, he was offered a job with the company.

Shortly after Sandy started the new job, his mother became ill. She was hospitalized for several months, then had to be placed in a nursing home. Sandy had been living alone in their small apartment for three years now despite encouragement from his boss to purchase property. Already in her seventies, Rose McPherson still had all her wits about her. She was sharp and bright and looked forward to weekly visits from her son as well as their daily conversations on the phone.

Sandy had confided in his mother. He told her about his love for Fiona but refrained from telling her too much about the girl he wanted to marry. He knew she would express some concern to know that Fiona was already a mother but more so to learn that she was only nineteen. Nevertheless, he decided to let her know about the baby and his plans to adopt him soon after the wedding. However, he had no intentions of mentioning Fiona's age. Rose McPherson always chided her son about getting married and starting a family, so Sandy was very hopeful that she would be delighted to know that he was going to have one sooner than she thought. On the other hand, John Leighton wanted his daughter to be married and was proud to have a son-in-law who could provide for her and his grandson. He was very disappointed and ashamed when Fiona could not continue college because she became pregnant. He thought that with her marriage to Sandy McPherson, he would no longer feel like a failure as a father.

Although John wanted desperately to know who the father of his grandchild was, he respected Fiona's silence and did not wish to cause further stress on his family by forcing her to admit that she was intimate with Stephen Brimm. Fiona was in love with Steve; she had hoped that he would have asked her to marry him when he found out about the pregnancy, and she was distraught when he discontinued their friendship. She kept hoping that he would change his mind, but after the birth of the baby and still no word from him, she lost hope. She was also aware that Steve did not mention any of this to his family. *How could he?* she thought. His parents would be angry with her. Steve was also ambitious and wanted to follow in his father's footsteps—to become an architectural engineer like him and take over the family business founded by his grandfather. Despite being in love with Steve, Fiona chose to start a new life for the sake of her baby son by marrying Sandy McPherson. Although she was not in love with him, she respected the young man and had started to become fond of him. To have a family of her own for the sake of her baby was all she hoped for. She was also aware that her marriage would make her parents happy and bring peace and harmony into their lives again. In a way, she was relieved that the Brimms did not know about the baby. They were a wealthy upper-class family with good connections, and Fiona came from a middle-class family with strong religious beliefs and a social life surrounded by family, close friends, and their church community.

It was a brisk autumn day in December. Her marriage to Sandy was just ten days away. Fiona was happy and anxious about the changes that would take place in her life. She prayed that it would all work out for the best and looked forward to her meeting with Sandy's mother whom she was visiting that afternoon. She dressed carefully, making sure to look smart and mature even though youth shone forth from her pretty face. Having stopped on the way to buy the best red roses in town, she held on to Sandy's arm as they entered the old lady's room at the nursing home.

"Hello, Mom, how is my best girl?" Sandy said as he hugged his mother; then he introduced his bride-to-be.

Rose was kind; she hugged and kissed Fiona and told her that she looked like a baby herself. Fiona smiled, and a blush came over her face that made her cheeks ruby red. Seeing her discomfort, Sandy put his arms around her and told his mother how much they were in love with each other and were hoping to have her blessing before they were married. Rose asked her son to give her some alone time with Fiona, insisting she had to get to know her better and suggesting that he go out to buy them some cookies.

"But you shouldn't have cookies," Sandy protested.

"I can have a few," she insisted.

He reluctantly left his bride-to-be in his mother's care and stepped out of the room. Not wanting to be away from them for too long, he looked at his watch and made a dash for the deli at the corner of the street. Fiona was afraid; she gave Sandy a wide-eyed glance before he left the room. She did not know what to expect from this seemingly charming older woman who looked more like her grandmother than her mother-in-law-to-be. She felt challenged by the overwhelming circumstances that appeared to have conspired on all fronts at that very moment. However, she took a deep breath and kept quite calm. Rose McPherson requested Fiona to move her chair closer to the bed. She then took the girl's hand, held it tightly, and said a quiet prayer. The old lady seemed quite composed as she started to tell Fiona all about the boyhood of the man she was going to marry. Fiona listened with rapt attention, managing a whimsical smile at the look of admiration on the face of the old lady as she spoke of her son, her only child.

"Do you know they told me I'll be childless?" she said with sternness in her voice. "It certainly took years, but I have the best son a mother could ever hope to have."

She looked at Fiona, searching her face to find some form of acknowledgment. Fiona nodded in agreement. She sat quietly and asked no questions. In fact, she was quite happy with the person her fiancé was and had no desire to enter into a discussion about him. She already knew he was a kindhearted, well-mannered, hardworking young man who was willing to give her a chance to have a good life for herself and baby.

Mama Rose, as she liked to be called, realized she was talking a lot about her son and wanted to hear from Fiona as well, so she asked her about the baby. She wanted to know how old he was and how well she was coping with him. But before Fiona could answer her questions, the door opened, and Sandy entered the room carrying a large box of cookies and some ice cream.

"I was just asking Fiona about the baby," his mother told him. "Maybe you can tell me about my new grandson too."

"Well," said Sandy, "he is the sweetest baby in the whole world, but I would prefer to let you be the judge of that when we bring him to see you next week. How's that?"

Fiona smiled, reached into her purse, pulled out a photo of the baby, and handed it to Mama Rose. "You may have this," she said. "We will bring you a photo frame the next time we visit."

The old lady looked long and hard at the photo. Then to break the silence, she asked Sandy when he was going to adopt him.

"I'm glad you asked," he said. "Soon after the wedding, we have already completed the paperwork."

Adoption of the baby was a simple, straightforward procedure. Fiona did not state on the birth record who the baby's father was, so the child only had one parent. Although she gave her son a name, Fiona and her family fondly called him Teddy.

It was late evening when the couple left the nursing home after a long and interesting visit with Mama Rose McPherson. They were both pleased and satisfied with themselves. Fiona felt more at ease with the woman who was going to be her mother-in-law than she did when she first met her. They felt more relaxed to forge ahead with their wedding plans and enjoyed the cold night air as they strolled hand in hand along the busy promenade. Sandy told Fiona all about his plans to purchase a small farm outside town. He said it was approximately seventy miles away from her parents' home and had a fairly large house with a garage and a barn on the property. The present owners were getting on in years and were forced to discontinue farming. They were looking forward to spending their twilight years with their children in Australia. He told her he would let her know more about it as soon as he gathered all the information concerning the sale of the property, which was—at that time—in the hands of his boss, Alfred Gunning.

Fiona knew that buying a farm meant that Sandy would have to quit working in the town. They would be living far away from her parents, and he would have to give up a good job to try his hand at farming—something they both knew nothing about. However, she trusted his judgment and knew he would do his best for her and the baby. She secretly pledged to help him with whatever he desired to accomplish. Fiona was somewhat relieved at the idea of having some distance between the town of Hillcrest and the place that would soon be her home. She asked Sandy if he had spent any time on a farm before.

"No," he said but told her that his parents lived quite close to a farm when he was a young child, and he still reminisced about the smell of farm life.

Fiona felt relieved when she heard of his intentions to retain most of the farmhands along with the present supervisor of planting and harvesting.

"I have to give it a lot of thought," he told her. "I will meet with Mr. Gunning and our attorneys as soon as the holidays are over. But for now, we will make my apartment our home after the wedding, if that is acceptable to you."

Fiona sighed, said that would be fine, and held on the Sandy's arm as they entered the gate to her home.

Chapter 4
Festive Times

On the eve of her wedding, Fiona woke up very early to feed the baby. And instead of going back to bed for a short nap, she decided to get busy with decorating the house for the occasion. She checked the to-do list her mother left on the kitchen table and tried to get most of it completed before her parents got out of bed. John Leighton took the day off from his job at Pembroke Bookstore where he worked for many years as a manager. Gerald came downstairs to help his sister, rubbing his eyes and yawning widely.

"Why are you up so early?" he inquired.

"Well, if you get moving, we will be finished in no time and could go back to bed before Mom and Dad come down," Fiona replied.

The two siblings worked quickly and quietly, and together they did a fantastic job of putting up all the decorations and arranging the chairs that the rental company delivered to their house the day before.

When John and Elsie came down for breakfast that morning, they were surprised that there was little to be done. Grandma Leighton followed them a few minutes after pulling the sashes of her dressing gown tightly around her and announcing that she had to have coffee before starting the chores. She headed straight for the kitchen, barely noticing how beautifully decorated the place was. Then as if something had alerted her, she stopped and, with a jerk of her head, surveyed the scene. Exclaiming that the house looked beautiful, she entered the kitchen to join the others.

It was a happy day for Elsie and her mother-in-law. They cooked, baked, and reminisced about the day John and Elsie were married. When all the chores were completed, they seasoned and prepared the meats that had to be cooked the next day, then arranged a small bouquet for Fiona. It was a quiet evening at the Leighton residence. The family decided not to put up the Christmas tree until after the wedding; nevertheless, the place still looked festive enough with the decorations that hung from the chandelier and streamers everywhere. With some satisfaction, they all decided to have an early night so they could be up bright and early the next morning. Gerald stayed up to help his sister while she completed last-minute packing.

"I think I have everything I need at this time for Teddy and me," Fiona said as she closed a large suitcase. "I can always come over for anything else I may need." She smiled at her brother with tears in her eyes.

Gerald folded a blanket nervously as he questioned his sister, "Will you be happy, Fiona?"

"Sure, I think so," she said and turned her back to him so he could not see the tears that had begun to roll down her pale cheeks. "Don't worry, I'll be happy," she said as if to convince herself.

"Will you visit often?" he asked.

"Yes!" she exclaimed. "You must also come and see us every chance you get."

"I will come," he said. "Sandy seems nice, maybe we can all go fishing sometime."

"I want you to take good care of Mom and Dad, and you must promise to let me know if they need me to do anything for them." Fiona continued, "I know they would not wish to bother us, but Sandy is a good guy, and I will be glad to help out wherever I could."

It was close to midnight when Fiona finally finished her packing. She checked the baby and turned off the light. Then pulling the covers over her, she hugged her pillow and said a prayer before drifting off to sleep.

Saturday morning came all too quickly. A soft sound of chatter filtered through the house that signaled the older Leightons were already awake. Everyone was rushing around getting ready for the early-morning ceremony, which was scheduled to take place at home. The justice of peace called to say he would be arriving at eleven o'clock in the morning since he had to make an urgent trip out of town. Elsie helped her daughter to get dressed, and Grandma Leighton took care of the baby. Aunt Violet arrived early, and John and Gerald helped her unload the car of all the food she had cooked. Sandy arrived at exactly ten o'clock, followed by Deacon Sam from their church. A few uncles, aunts, and cousins had begun to arrive while the deacon was gathering everyone for an opening prayer. The justice of peace arrived precisely at eleven and took his place next to the deacon. Gerald started the music as John waited at the foot of the stairs for his daughter, who began making her way out of her room at the top.

The ceremony was short and touching. Fiona looked angelic; Sandy beamed with pride. Elsie and Grandma Leighton were both teary eyed as they kissed and congratulated the new couple. Champagne was served, and everyone toasted the bride and groom. After a sumptuous luncheon, Sandy and Fiona thanked the relatives for being there and then excused themselves as they were about to leave for their honeymoon. Grandma and Grandpa Leighton extended their visit for two more days to help out with the baby until the couple returned.

Christmas was a few days away when Sandy and Fiona started their lives as husband and wife in Sandy's small apartment. There was much to be done to convert it from a bachelor's quarters to a home for a couple with a baby. However, they quickly got to work on moving, fixing, and redecorating and had it all ready in time for the holidays, complete with a Christmas tree as well as new drapes. When they finished the apartment, John, Elsie, and Gerald were invited over for a toast on Christmas Eve. The next day, Sandy and Fiona had Christmas dinner with the family after visiting Mama Rose at the nursing home.

Soon after the holidays, Sandy completed the adoption of the baby. They named him Rhoyan Andrew McPherson. Sandy cared for the child as if it were his own son. He promised Fiona to do his best to make life happy and comfortable for them.

Early in the new year, Sandy saw the need to speed up his purchase of the Selby farm before the opportunity slipped away from him. He discussed this with Alfred Gunning who was delighted to assist him with the proceedings. Mr. Gunning, however, lamented the fact that he was going to lose a good employee and had to find a suitable replacement for Sandy in his tax office. As soon as the formalities and inspections of the farm were completed, a closing date was fixed to finalize the purchase.

Chapter 5
The Challenge

After five months in a small apartment, Fiona was relieved to relocate to a much larger home where the baby had a nursery and more room to grow and play. He was one year old at the time, having moved just after celebrating his first birthday. Although a bit sad to live farther away from her parents and brother, Fiona knew she could see them as often as she wanted. She had no time to feel lonely as there was much to be done around the house.

The Selbys kept a clean and tidy home, which they had repainted just before the sale of the farm, so all that was left to be done was to have it fully furnished. The house was left with a large dining table and ten chairs along with an old wood-burning stove, which was used to heat the family room as well as keep the kettles warm. While Fiona made a day-to-day list of what was needed for the home, did the cooking, and looked after the baby, Sandy spent his time going over the books and particulars of the farm. He was also learning all about the crops from Angus Chapman, who managed the farm for the Selbys and agreed to stay on to assist Sandy with the transition.

"It is hard work but very rewarding," Angus told the young couple.

Nevertheless, they were happy and contented and determined to make a success of it. Sandy had a bit of savings that he set aside to assist them until the farm picked up again.

Spring was quite mild that year and facilitated the many changes and renovations that were done to the barn and sheds. Sandy made sure to stay on top of all that had to be completed and attended the farmers' meetings so he could acquaint himself with other farmers and learn about any problems that might arise in the district.

Their first summer on the farm came quickly, bringing with it longer days and shorter nights. Sandy woke up early, before dawn, every day to meet with Angus Chapman who was always in the barn before the crack of dawn. He usually took a flask of coffee with him, and the two discussed the day's work over a hot cup. Although Angus consulted Sandy on everything, he was pretty much in charge of the day-to-day running of the farm. The work was evenly distributed among the farmhands that Sandy retained. Angus inspected the crops and fields as well as supervised the farmhands. Sandy usually accompanied him to gather knowledge. However, he set aside some of his day to spend in his home office, reconciling his books and marketing his produce.

Sandy and Fiona were both disappointed that they could not visit Mama Rose every weekend as they usually did. They called her daily and always gave her the latest updates on farm life as well as what was new with the baby. Fiona's parents visited as often as they could. Elsie helped her daughter with redecorating the house whenever she could and even took her furniture-shopping at the old mills furniture barn situated a few miles away, where Fiona was able to get most of her furniture. The house was large—three bedrooms on the second floor and one on the first floor, which was specially added to accommodate the aged Selbys. By the end of summer, it was mostly furnished. All the floors were scrubbed, and fresh drapes hung from every window.

It had been just over three months since the couple moved to Meadowbrook Farm. They had fully settled in, and the farm was running smoothly with the help of Angus Chapman. On a bright summer Saturday morning, Sandy woke up very early as usual and whispered to Fiona that he wanted to travel to Hillcrest to see his mother that day. They decided to make the trip quite early so they could enjoy a long visit with Mama Rose. It was ten o'clock in the morning when they arrived at the nursing home. The old lady was happy to see her son and daughter-in-law. She played with the baby as he sat snuggly on her lap and sang to him softly while rocking him back and forth.

Before traveling back to the farm, they made a brief stop in the early afternoon to see John and Elsie Leighton. Fiona was excited to see her old neighborhood again. It was the first time she had been there since moving to the farm. She was somehow a bit rigid as they approached the house because she caught a glimpse of the boy who rode past them on his bicycle and knew that it was Steve Brimm's younger brother Albert. Fiona had no desire to see any of the Brimms for the rest of her life and hated the fact that they lived in the neighborhood as well.

The trip back to the farm was pleasant; the air was dry. A cool wind blew across the meadows that made the trees sway to and fro. Upon arrival, Angus reported to Sandy that a storm was in the forecast for the next day, so the two men got busy putting away the machinery in the barn while Fiona hurried inside to feed the baby. *It was an enjoyable summer,* she thought to herself as she stood in the middle of the room, staring out the window at the men as they moved the equipment into the barn. Taking a deep breath and savoring the fresh farm air, she filled up her lungs and let it all out with a loud sigh. She kept her eyes focused on Sandy as he struggled to close the barn door against the breeze and wondered when she started to feel the way she did about him. She could not explain it and did not know when it all happened. She had begun to look at him as her husband instead of the friend she married. Her thoughts were suddenly interrupted by the baby's cries. She turned, picked up the bottle she had prepared, and went off to feed him.

Before the end of summer, most of the family had paid a visit to the farm. Some brought gifts for the home and took back baskets of fruits and vegetables. Angus's wife offered to teach Fiona to preserve fruit for the winter. She helped her convert part of their basement into storage with racks for all sizes of jars. It had become difficult for Sandy and Fiona to leave the farm on weekends. There was always something to be done even though Angus was there to welcome visiting customers who stopped by from time to time. However, they tried to exchange visits with new friends from neighboring farms and enjoyed many warm quiet nights by themselves sitting on the old porch swing, basking in the moonlight.

It was just over six months since they began running the farm. The harvest was good, and Sandy was somewhat surprised that he was able to keep his head above water at his first crop season. He had Angus to thank for that and conveyed his appreciation. Fiona was not excited about the coming winter as much as she was about the summer that had gone by. The fall colors were breathtaking in the country, unlike anything that was seen in the small town of Hillcrest where she lived before. The leaves were now mostly all gone, along with their bright colors, and took with them her enthusiasm for farm life.

Another Thanksgiving was approaching, and Fiona thought she could try her hand at making dinner for the whole family. That would give her something to look forward to as the days grew short and dreary. Her parents would have to spend the holiday at the farm. That thought sent a bit of excitement through her. She wanted to include her grandparents and Aunt Violet as well but felt she should speak to her mother about it since she would need her help with preparations and cooking. She wasted no time in doing so. Elsie was proud of her daughter for undertaking such an enormous task at that stage of her young married life. Needless to say, everyone was excited about the idea, especially Gerald who missed his sister and baby nephew.

Fiona thought it would take a bit of planning to get everyone out to the farm for Thanksgiving that year. She knew it would have been near impossible to get Mama Rose to be there and did not give it another thought. However, she had to encourage her mother to spend a few days before the holiday to assist with baking and preparations. Elsie obliged and traveled out to the farm two days before, leaving her husband and son to join her. Angus's wife pitched in to help, and together the ladies baked several pumpkin, strawberry, and peach pies along with rye bread, which was shared out to the workers on the farm. It was an enjoyable Thanksgiving. Grandma and Grandpa Leighton did not go to their daughter's that year as they preferred to visit the farm. They traveled with John and Gerald while Aunt Violet took a bus. They all arrived at noon and had a wonderful country holiday.

Chapter 6
Raising a Family

Having become seasoned farmers as the years rolled by, Fiona made life as pleasant as she could for her family. On occasion, her mind would wander to her youthful life in Hillcrest, especially when she looked at young Roy, as he was called. He reminded her so much of Steve Brimm. At twenty-six, she had three children. Her second son, Rory, was blond, and her daughter, Roseanne, had red hair like Fiona; but Roy had dark-brown hair like Steve. He was born with a tiny scar on his right hip that began to grow as he got older. Fiona was worried that it would not stop growing. She took him to a local hospital to have it checked out when he was five years old and was relieved to learn that it was only a birthmark.

Even though the children enjoyed farm life, they looked forward to the occasional trip to Hillcrest to visit their grandparents. It was on one of these visits that the two boys had a strange encounter with Mrs. Brimm. Roy and Rory were playing on the sidewalk with a wooden scooter their Uncle Gerald made for them when they accidentally rolled into the middle-aged woman. She had just come from a house on that block where she was visiting an elderly relative who had been ill. The incident startled her, and she glared at the boys who almost knocked her off her feet. They were terrified as they sat sprawled flat on the sidewalk.

Roy, who was seven years old at that time, managed to scramble to his feet and say, "Pardon me, ma'am, my brother did not see you coming. His head was down."

"But you certainly did!" she scolded him. "Ah! Never mind!" She brushed off her frock and continued on her way.

The boys stared at her until she turned the corner; then, picking up the scooter, they ran as fast as they could into the house. Their grandmother had been sitting near a window, knitting and keeping an eye on them as usual when they played outside. She saw the whole incident from the opening in the curtain but refrained from scolding the boys about their recklessness. Instead, she made them wash their faces and hands and poured them each a glass of warm milk. Elsie had always been suspicious about Roy's bloodline. She observed how nervous her daughter became whenever the Brimm name was mentioned. Even though seven years had passed, Fiona never wanted to talk about her teenage pregnancy, not even with her husband. "Such things are better left unsaid," was her reply whenever the question came up. "Sandy is his father, and he has no other," she once told her mother. Ever since then, Elsie was careful never to talk about it.

Mama Rose McPherson had been ailing for quite a few months and had to be admitted to Hillcrest Memorial Hospital. After a few days there, she developed pneumonia and passed away. Sandy was heartbroken. His only consolation was knowing that she was able to enjoy her grandchildren, especially Roseanne who was named for her.

Not long after her demise, the family felt another loss. Fiona's grandparents, who were certainly getting on in years, passed away within one year of each other. They were in their late eighties. That was indeed a hard year for the Leighton/McPherson families. They rallied on, immersing themselves in work and family life. The year that followed, Sandy decided to take a gamble with the changing of crops. He also made some investments that he hoped would bring him good yields in a timely fashion.

The farm did better than he had expected, given the harsh winters and blistering summer days that followed what turned out to be bad investments, as well as the uncertainty of the crops. Angus Chapman had retired after spending ten more years assisting Sandy with the farm. He did not intend to stay that long when the young couple arrived, but he formed such a bond with them that he made sure Sandy knew all he needed to know before retiring. The Chapmans regarded the young couple as the children they always wanted. Even though Sandy missed not having Angus around, he was doing a great job of managing the farm himself.

At seventeen, Roy was a great help to his father. He loved farming but also loved his books. He was an excellent student who made the honor roll every year, and Sandy was very proud of him. Roy was quite gifted as well; he learned everything he could about tractors so he could maintain the ones on the farm after Angus left. He even overhauled an old one, which Sandy thought was beyond repair, and had it working as good as new.

There were now five children in the McPherson household, Fiona having given birth to two more sons: Raymond, called Ray, who was nine, and Ralph, fondly called Ralphie. At six, he was the baby of the family. Although Sandy had three more sons, he spent a lot of time with Roy who was always in his father's shadow, whether he was looking after machinery in the barn or out in the fields.

Sandy loved all his children, but he had a special fondness for Roy, something which Fiona could not explain but was grateful for. She sometimes wondered what her life would have been like had she not agreed to marry Sandy. She always wanted to further her studies and dreamed of becoming a teacher when she was in high school. However, life had taken her down a different path, and Fiona was through with lamenting. Because Sandy was a lot older, she relied on him heavily when they were first married. To her, he was a father figure, and she admired him for it. But as the years went by, her love for him grew; and with each new birth, she became more assertive. They were now true partners. Fiona made all the decisions concerning the family and household while Sandy ran the farm.

Because her homemade jams and preserves were always a big hit at their church fair, Fiona decided to make a business of it and pooled all her efforts into having a regular supply for friends, neighbors, and visitors to the farm. In the winters when there was little canning to be done, she knitted hats, scarves, and gloves for her family. She made sure that all the children had some chores to do and saw to it that homework was completed and studying done. Sandy never intervened where these things were concerned; he knew that Fiona was in full control. Although he was lenient with Roy, he never failed to discipline him when necessary and made sure that the same treatment was meted out to all his children.

It was a cold winter day in early March, and Roy had been late in coming home from school that afternoon, so Sandy moved the truck and ploughed into the barn with some help from Rory, who was fifteen years old at that time. After he had done so, he left the boy to close the barn doors and put on the latches. Sandy was approaching the house when he heard a frightful scream. Not seeing Rory anywhere, he called out to Fiona and ran back to the barn only to find his son sitting on the hay with a pitchfork stuck in his foot. He summoned an ambulance, then removed the fork after tying the boy's leg with his mother's apron.

Roy returned home shortly after his brother was taken to the hospital and was told about the incident. He dropped his books and hitched a ride there, arriving just in time to see Rory being released on a pair of crutches. Roy loved his brother; he was very protective of him and was petrified at the thought of him losing his leg. However, that was not the case as he found out when he saw him wobbling out of the emergency room at the cottage hospital center. Sandy was relieved to see Roy, but Fiona scolded him for being late. The worried parents spent hours at the small hospital with their injured son, but having received a favorable prognosis, they were anxious to take him home.

Roy carried his brother on his back up the stairs to his room. He felt guilty for being late in coming home, mainly because his father never asked for an explanation. He spent the next ten days tending to Rory's wound. Every day, he changed dressings, cleaned, and bandaged his brother's foot with such precision that the nurses complimented him when he accompanied Rory to have his sutures removed.

"I think you would make an excellent doctor," the head nurse told Roy.

"Well, I was thinking of making it my career, but I still have a long way to go before med school," he replied.

Rory gave his brother a cheerful smile. "Don't worry, you'll make it," he said. "But first, you'll have to help me with my wooden legs."

"Stay put, I'll see if Dad is up front." Roy hurried to the front entrance. Seeing the pickup, he ran back to assist his brother.

On the way home, Rory spoke about his brother's enthusiasm for medicine. Sandy always thought Roy would be an engineer. One can just imagine his surprise to learn that the boy wanted to become a doctor.

"That would take some hard work," he told his son. "I would have to save more to be able to afford medical school, with the others to think about as well. You would need to get a scholarship or two,"

"Well, Dad, I'm working on it," Roy replied as the truck stopped in the driveway.

"When did you decide on becoming a doctor?" Sandy asked as he rubbed Roy's head and gave him a soft hug.

"I don't know, I guess I always dreamed of being a doctor. Maybe because of my passion for science," the boy continued.

"What about engineering?" his father asked.

"Oh, that's just a hobby," he said, and they laughed as they hopped out of the pickup truck and headed for the stairs.

"What about me, guys? Don't forget me!" Rory shouted as he grabbed his crutches and waited for his brother to assist him. "Did you forget why you are having this conversation? It's all about *me*."

He teased, "Point taken, old chap."

Sandy sighed and carefully lifted his son out of the truck while Roy reached for the crutches. "I hope there's something special for lunch." "Any more special treatment and I won't be able to lift you," his father mumbled as he placed his son gently on the porch.

Fiona was amused to see her husband and sons stumbling into the house in such good spirits. Rose had been helping her mother all day with cookie-baking for their local Easter fair. She barely looked up at the boys when they stormed into the kitchen, driven by the sweet smells that permeated the atmosphere. Rose was pampered by her brothers, but she was not prepared to share any of the cookies with them. With Ray and Ralphie out in the barn feeding and grooming the old pony, she pretty much enjoyed having the kitchen to herself and dreaded the intrusion.

It was an eventful weekend for the family. Fiona took Rose and Ralphie to the Easter fair while Sandy and his three older sons visited the local cinema. Gerald and his wife made a surprise visit to the farm and arrived late that Saturday evening. He had not seen his sister and family in more than a year and particularly wanted to spend some time with his niece and nephews before Roy went off to college. It had been three years since he was married and moved to Boston to play with the Philharmonic. This was very demanding on his time as he had to do quite a bit of traveling. The children were excited to see their uncle and aunt, especially Roy who was keen to know more about Boston since he was hoping to gain acceptance to Harvard.

"I'm keeping my fingers crossed that my grades would help me gain entry," he confessed.

"Well, my boy, I promise to be back for your graduation!" Gerald shouted with an exuberance that captivated his nephews.

"Then we'll be seeing you again in two months?" Fiona asked in disbelief.

"Sure!" he replied. His wife cupped her cheeks with both hands and nodded; her uncertainty resonated with simplicity.

Fiona looked forward to seeing her brother soon again and, most notably, getting better acquainted with her sister-in-law.

While they all made plans for Gerald's subsequent visit, Roy thought of nothing else but the daily mail. Graduation day was fast approaching, and there still was no reply from the university of his choice, although he gained admission to a few others. He had already been awarded two scholarships and several bursaries—all of which delighted his parents—but Roy was disheartened. A lot of pressure had been placed on him by Mr. Trots, his high school principal, to choose one of these scholarships. However, with encouragement from his father, Roy deferred that decision until after graduation.

That day arrived before he was quite ready for it, or so he thought. The sun shone brightly on the spacious lawns of Bingham High. The class of '77 looked stunning in their shiny satin blue gowns and caps with gold tassels. His grandparents, along with Aunt Violet and Uncle Gerald, attended the graduation with the family. Roy was valedictorian, an excellent student who graduated at the top of his class and was well respected by his classmates. Sandy and Fiona were so proud of their son they agreed to grant him the only request he made—a graduation party for all his friends. So they hired a small hall for the event.

Two days after graduation, Roy received the letter he was hoping for all spring. It took a long time in coming, but the news was worth waiting for. He gained acceptance to Harvard University with full scholarship. It was a bittersweet moment for Fiona; she was thrilled for her son but felt sad at the thought of letting him go. She thought she was going to miss him more than anyone else; she did not even consider how Sandy might feel when he heard the news. He had loved Roy more than she had expected. Father and son shared many moments together. Sandy was the first one to teach Roy to ride a bicycle, to fish, to play pool, to drive a tractor, and more importantly, to read when he was just three years old. Sure he was going to miss him, but he was also looking forward to sending his son to an Ivy League college.

It took Fiona two weeks to finalize all the arrangements for her son's graduation party. He had already prepared a list of friends he wanted to invite, along with the name of a DJ who played music for their school prom. His mother did not let that evening go by without being present to keep an eye on things and made sure the teens had enough to eat. Rory and Rose were allowed to attend their brother's party. Sandy and two of his friends from the parent/teachers' association agreed to supervise the teens that evening, making sure that no alcohol was sneaked into the premises. Fiona kept a keen eye on her son without being too obvious, mainly because she thought there might be someone special who captured his attention. Events of a similar night many years ago flooded her memory. She was determined not to let her son make the same mistake. Consequently, before the event, she encouraged Sandy to have a talk with him.

After a beautiful evening of fun and disco dancing, parents collected their children, and the family returned to the farm. Fiona was a bit curious; she saw quite a few girls at the party but could not identify anyone who seemed special to Roy.

"Did you have a girlfriend at the party?" she asked him when they arrived home.

He blushed and then, with a short reply, said, "Nope."

"Why not?" his mother questioned.

Just then, the phone rang and Roy rushed to answer it. Slumping in an armchair near the phone, he made himself comfortable for a long conversation, hoping his mother would be in bed before he was through. Fiona later learned from Sandy that her son's girlfriend relocated with her parents to California a week before the party, and she was going to attend UCLA.

Gerald was excited to hear the news of his nephew's acceptance to Harvard and wasted no time in offering him a place to stay in his home. Both Gerald and his wife, Liz, were accomplished musicians who had no children at that time, so they were glad to have their nephew stay with them. However, it was a choice Roy had to make. He had looked forward to living on campus, but his uncle's offer seemed to put a damper on his enthusiasm. Having had many conversations about it with his mother, who thought her brother's offer was a good idea, Roy appealed to the better judgment of his father.

Sandy always stood up for his son. He fully understood his situation. He thought Roy should experience the full effects of college life without having to be monitored and taken care of on a daily basis. As a result, he had a talk with Gerald who also understood his nephew's desire to live on campus. Although a bit disappointed, he nevertheless left the option open for Roy to spend his weekends with them whenever he felt homesick. The problem was convincing Fiona that living on campus was good for her son, and that task was left up to Sandy. It took some doing, but in the end, Fiona agreed that it would be good for her son to be independent.

It was the McPherson family's turn to host the annual Fourth of July picnic that year, and Sandy wanted it to be special. He dug a large pit and prepared it to roast a suckling pig and invited all the relatives so everyone could say good-bye to Roy before he left the farm. The family was particularly happy to see Angus and his wife again. They had not seen much of them since Angus retired seven years ago. Fiona noticed that Rory seemed to be the only one not having a good time. While the others were enjoying the outdoor cooking and finishing the apple cider, Rory sat quietly on the porch with his grandfather. He was in a pensive mood; the thought of his brother being away from him made him sad. The two boys were inseparable, but Rory loved farm life more than Roy did. He wondered what would happen to him when his turn came for college. It was something he had not given much thought to before, and that time was fast approaching.

Summer vacation was all too short for Rory and Roy; it was August, and Roy was going off to college. Sandy rented a large van to accommodate the entire family along with Roy's luggage, which included lots of food supplies, an iron, an electric kettle, detergent, and a few cooking utensils. "Just in case you have something to cook," his mother warned. They all made the trip to Boston very early Friday morning and arrived at Gerald's house after several hours.

The family had never been there before. Liz was a gracious host; she had beds set up in the family room to accommodate the children while Sandy and Fiona occupied the guest room. The next morning, after a good old-fashioned breakfast, Sandy and Fiona set out with Roy for the university. He hugged and kissed his sister and brothers and promised to write whenever he had the time.

"Don't miss me too much," he told Rose as he pulled her ponytails. "I'll be home again for Thanksgiving."

"Call whenever you need me to get you," Gerald told his nephew as he tapped him on his back. Roy nodded, then Sandy shifted the gear, and the van reversed through the gate.

A surge of pride came over Sandy as he drove away from the campus, waving at his son who stood at his dorm window looking rather dazed and managing a faint grin as he waved back. Fiona's painted smile could not hide the tears that had begun to roll down her cheeks. The drive back to the farm on that sunny Sunday morning seemed much longer. The children were not as talkative, and no one cared to stop for lunch on the way. So Sandy just relaxed, turned on the radio, and hit the gas for a speedy drive home.

Rory felt the emptiness of the room he shared with his older brother. He wondered about attending college as well and thought that if he could also make it to Harvard, then he would be near Roy. That thought made him realize that he needed to work harder at gaining a scholarship to the prestigious school. Although it was Roy who repaired the tractors and hung around his father all the time, Rory was the one who seemed more interested in farming, especially with regards to weather patterns and its effect on production. He was always the encouraging one when his father wanted to invest in new crops. He however realized that he was two years away from graduating high school and still was unsure of what he wanted as a career.

Chapter 7
A New Love

Soon enough with the passage of time, the three older children were off to college, and the homestead was left with only Ray and Ralphie. At fifteen years old, Ray was his father's little "man of business" while Ralphie preferred running errands for his mother. Rory had just finished his undergrad studies and remained an extra year at college to complete his master's. He had set his mind on returning to the farm to run the business. Roy was in his final stage at medical school, and the family seldom got to see him as he only came home for Thanksgiving and Christmas holidays. However, Rose returned home every chance she got since she enjoyed being treated like a queen by her two younger brothers.

Fiona's parents, Elsie and John Leighton, were certainly getting on in years. Her Aunt Violet was not as active as she used to be since having arthritis. She could not attend most of the family functions and missed the opportunity of seeing Roy graduate medical school because of a broken ankle. Nevertheless, she was able to be present at Rory's graduation. Aunt Violet was the live wire in the family. Being widowed at an early age with no children of her own, she considered her sister's children as her own daughter and son. Violet was particularly happy that life had turned out so wonderfully for her niece who shared her sentiments. She had five beautiful children and a husband she loved as much as he loved her. The farm was doing quite well, and her canning business took off and was holding its own because of a growing demand for her homemade jams and jellies.

Fiona refused to let her mind stray to thoughts of her younger years or even think of Stephen Brimm, especially since as he got older, Roy looked nothing like the boy she once knew. Likewise, Steve was a successful engineer who, having completed his education, joined his father's firm of engineers and quickly rose to the top when his father retired. He was CEO of a successful firm, married, and had two daughters. He had long forgotten his own graduation party when he was a boy and never gave a thought to the girl who told him of her dilemma when they were only eighteen years old. Their lives had taken separate paths, and the common bond they shared was no longer an issue for Fiona as she was the only one who carried that secret.

During his internship, Roy was on call almost seven days a week, and what little time he had left was spent with his grandparents reviving for the next day. Because he chose to do his internship at Hillcrest Memorial Hospital, Elsie and John Leighton saw their grandson more than his parents did. He, however, called them often and intermittently visited the farm during the year. Fiona was not at all bothered when Roy announced that he had chosen to do his internship at Hillcrest Hospital. In fact, she was happy to know that he was close by to keep an eye on his grandparents since her weekly trips to see them were no longer as frequent as she would have liked. Because it was convenient for him, Roy resided close to the hospital, and the distance to his grandparents was also a short one. Nevertheless, he made sure to call ahead before he visited so Grandma Elsie could prepare his favorite dish.

After graduate studies, Rose returned to Meadowbrook and taught at the local middle school she once attended. Rory decided to stay on the farm to manage the new canning company and help his father with the business aspects of the farm. Ray was hoping to get a job in the city with a firm of auditors after he completed all his accounting exams, for which he was studying diligently, and Ralphie felt proud to follow in his brother's footsteps when he entered college at Fennimore.

It did not take long for Elsie Leighton to realize that after three years of regular visits, she did not see her grandson quite as often, although he called his Grandpa John every day to remind him to take his medication. Whenever Roy found time to visit, his grandmother chided him about not caring for an old lady's cooking anymore, so he decided to surprise them with a special visit on a cool Sunday afternoon in the spring of '89. He arrived accompanied by the love of his life, a young lady he met two years before at a medical conference. They became good friends and saw each other as often as time permitted. Trudy Wilkins did research for a pharmaceutical company, and her work involved a bit of traveling. She was quite tiny for her twenty-seven years but had a winning smile and a charming personality that made the old lady like her right away.

The visit was enjoyable; Elsie Leighton prepared her special dessert and homemade fruit punch, and Grandpa John brought out a bottle of his oldest wine to have a toast. When he was leaving, Roy gave his grandmother a big hug, and she slipped a note into his pocket. He discreetly looked at it as he closed the car door for Trudy, who was already comfortably seated on the passenger side. A cute frown framed his boyish face as he waved good-bye and shouted, "I'll let you know, Grandma!" The car roared as he sped away, and Roy thought to himself that he was now obliged to introduce his girlfriend to his parents and the rest of the family.

In the days that followed, he arranged a weekend with Trudy for them to visit the farm. Fiona was quite excited to meet the girl who had captured her son's heart. She heard from her mother all about Trudy and had mixed feelings about the visit. Nevertheless, she was determined to make it a pleasant one. Two days before they arrived, Fiona converted Ralphie's room into a guest room for Trudy. She was well received by the family and was a big hit with Ralphie, who never failed to ask if his room was comfortable enough for her. Despite her reservations, Fiona was quite impressed. She expected Roy to tell her more about his feelings for the girl, but he did not. Having his girlfriend meet the family meant that he was pretty serious about the relationship, and his mother was comfortable with that. Rose discovered that she shared a common interest with Trudy: they both enjoyed arts and craft, and the two spent most of the weekend sharing their skills.

Sandy and Roy took a moonlit stroll after Sunday evening dinner to get ice cream for the family from a convenience shop nearby. It was a long walk, and the two were able to have an interesting father-son conversation on the way. Roy confided in his father that he was going to propose to Trudy shortly after meeting her parents. Sandy was happy for his son and promised not to spill the beans before the announcement.

When they returned home, the ice cream was a bit soft. Fiona glared at Sandy who merely shrugged his shoulders and smiled at his son, and the two disappeared from the room before anything was said. Both father and son realized they should have taken the car as they were going for ice cream. However, the cool temperature of a spring evening, along with a brightly lit moon and a yearning for fresh country air, compelled them to take their time in returning with the frozen dessert. The two were so wrapped up in conversation that they were completely oblivious of the contents of the brown paper bag they were carrying. Sandy enjoyed having a heart-to-heart talk with his son. It had been quite a long time since they had such an opportunity, and they both were carried away by it. Roy missed his father very much; however, his busy schedule did not allow for much time to be spent at the farm. Moreover, what little free time he had was ordained for Trudy.

Fiona knew there was a strong bond between Sandy and Roy, but she did not think it could have gotten any stronger, especially since they only saw their son occasionally now that he had a life of his own. She noted, with a tinge of jealously, how chummy father and son were as they embraced each other and chatted for a long time while the car engine purred after Roy had turned on the ignition in preparation for their return journey. She was so engrossed in her thoughts, as she stood on the porch to watch the couple leave, that she did not even notice the two strong arms that coiled around her shoulders and the chin that rested gently on the top of her head—as Rory often did.

When she finally came out of her trance, Fiona looked up at Rory and patted his cheeks. She knew she was being a bit selfish. After all, she had three other sons who also meant the world to her, and it was silly to want to monopolize Roy's affections. He was a well-grounded young man with an important career, and that was attributed to her and Sandy. Fiona knew there was something about Roy that no one could touch. Only she held the key to that special link, but the time was approaching when she would have to let go completely and allow him to make those significant choices she had dreaded for many years.

The year 1990 was filled with many happy events for the family. Roy's marriage to Trudy was held in the spring, and in the summer, Rose got engaged to the son of Mayor Bradford, who she had been friendly with since her college days. At ten years of age, Gerald's only son, Dane, was selected to give a guest appearance with a European philharmonic orchestra. He was an accomplished violinist, and everyone was excited about his tour, especially his grandparents and Aunt Fiona. It was a pity that none of them got to see any of Dane's performances because he lived in Boston, where it all happened. However, on rare occasions when the families all got together for one of the Leighton's special birthday celebrations—such as a sixty, seventy, or in the case of John, a seventy-fifth birthday—they got to hear him play for his grandparents.

After graduating with a degree in banking and finance, Ralphie was able to get a job with a bank in the city. Roy helped his brothers secure an apartment together as Raymond and Ralphie worked within blocks of each other, so both boys moved away from home and the farm. Fiona knew it was just a matter of time when Rose would be married, and the farm would only be left with Rory. She hated the thought; it made her feel as though her world would fall apart. She had built her life around her family, and it seemed as if it was all going to unravel. Furthermore, her fears were soon a reality when Rose and Michael Bradford announced to their parents that they were planning their wedding the following summer.

As the children were all well educated and had started life on their own, Sandy thought of selling the farm and just holding on to the canning business, but Fiona convinced him to keep it for Rory since he was the only one of her children interested in farming. Roy and Trudy settled in the town of Hillcrest because he preferred to continue his work with the hospital there. Trudy quit her job with the pharmaceutical company when she gave birth to their first child, and so that part of the family had once again gravitated to the town of their origin.

Chapter 8
A Strange Encounter

Life was not without its ups and downs for Fiona and her family. Her father was hospitalized after he suffered a severe stroke, which left him with many complications. Roy made sure he had the best team of doctors caring for his grandfather. He stopped by to check on him every morning and in the evening, when he was finished with his rounds. The family kept a constant vigil at the hospital in the first critical days but thereafter relied on Roy for constant updates on John Leighton, especially when Fiona returned to Meadowbrook. Elsie was in a state of distress over her husband's illness but found some consolation in the fact that he was receiving the best of care and treatment.

During one of his routine visits to the floor to see his grandfather, Roy was called away by a colleague for a consultation on a patient. Dr. Harmon often sought advice from Roy. He trusted his judgment and admired him for being a brilliant doctor. When Roy entered the room, the patient, a middle-aged man about fifty years, was propped up in bed examining the contents of the dinner tray in front of him. Dr. Harmon introduced Dr. McPherson, and the two doctors spoke briefly while looking at the patient's chart. Then Roy proceeded to examine Mr. Brimm. While doing so, he noticed that the patient had a scar on his right hip. He questioned him about it and was told that it was a birthmark.

"Quite a unique mark," Roy said. "I have only seen one other." And with that, he smiled and looked at the chart again, this time making note of the patient's name.

After a brief conversation with Dr. Harmon as they walked down the corridor, Roy departed to check on his grandfather. The next day, Dr. Harmon informed Roy that his patient's lab results were in, and he wanted to go over them with Roy at his earliest convenience. As usual, Roy always made himself available as soon as his busy schedule permitted. He however caught up with Dr. Harmon sooner than he had expected and was privileged to examine and give his opinion of the results concerning the patient who was diagnosed with a rare blood disorder.

"Would you allow me to do some further testing?" Roy inquired of his colleague.

"Sure, let me know if you come up with anything else," the good doctor replied.

So Roy put through the order for more lab work to be done on Mr. Brimm. He was particularly interested in his case and was not at all curious when he noticed that the patient had a similar blood type to his.

In keeping with his promise to his wife, Roy took his family out to the farm that weekend. It had been several weeks since he had taken his son to visit his parents. Fiona was thrilled to have a baby in the family after many years but expressed disappointment at not seeing her grandson often. While there, Roy mentioned to his father about his encounter with a scarred-hip patient at the hospital, and his mother overheard it.

"I found it a bit humorous," Roy said, and the two looked at each other and smiled.

A funny feeling came over Fiona, and she acted instinctively, sending Sandy out to check on the barbeque that was on the grill in the backyard and pulling Roy aside to help her move a table. When she was sure no one else could hear, Fiona questioned her son on what she had overheard.

"Oh, it was just something I mentioned to Dad because it seemed so unlikely. I really shouldn't discuss patients, Mom, just forget what you heard."

But Fiona could not forget. She knew she had to get Roy's attention, so against her better judgment, when she had the opportunity, she said to him softly, "Tell me, Roy, is the name of the patient Brimm by any chance?"

Roy's eyebrows rose as he gave his mother a questioning glance. "Why, what do you know about him?"

Fiona did not meet her son's gaze; instead, she turned her back to him and said, "There is something you should know about him."

Just then, Trudy came into the room to let them know that dinner was ready.

Sandy brought in the meat he was cooking on the grill and placed the dish on the table. Apart from Roy, no one else noticed that Fiona was quite uncomfortable during the meal. She scarcely ate, and her cheeks were pale. Roy asked his mother if she was feeling ill.

"No," she replied. "I'll just go and relax for a while on the porch. Maybe I need some fresh air."

After dinner, everyone joined Fiona on the porch and had ice cream. Soon the day was over, and having said their good-byes, Roy and his family returned to Hillcrest.

On Monday, Roy called his mother to see how she was doing and to give her an update on his grandfather whom he had seen that morning. Fiona was expecting the call; she told him she was feeling fine. "Just a little perturbed about Granddad," she said.

"Well, he is having the best care," Roy assured her.

"And what about old Mr. Brimm? Did he have a stroke too?" Fiona uttered abruptly.

"Mother, you are relentless!" Roy exclaimed. Then noticing the silence, he chuckled as he added, "Well, he is not that old. However, Mom, is there something you need to tell me?"

"Yes!" Fiona shouted. "And if I don't do this now, I would never get around to it."

"What is it?" Roy questioned.

His mother sighed, then told him she had to have a talk with him. "Could you come out to the farm alone on Friday evening? Dad and Rory will be off to see the pool tournament, and Rose will be at the movies with Michael."

"Will do, I'll arrange it," Roy agreed.

Fiona breathed a sigh of relief; she would have enough time to think of what she was going to say to her son. She wanted to keep it to herself and had no intentions of discussing it with Sandy before she had a chance to tell Roy what she felt he needed to know.

Whenever he checked on his grandfather, Roy made it his duty to stop by Mr. Brimm's room to ask how he was. He met with Dr. Harmon to discuss the results of the tests he had done on the man and promised to be available for consultation when needed. That Thursday morning, Roy was asked by Dr. Harmon to check the status of his patient and to let him know his opinion. So before visiting his grandfather, he called on Mr. Brimm. He entered the room to find a woman arranging flowers in a vase.

"Good morning, Mr. Brimm, lovely flowers," Roy said.

"Good morning, Dr. McPherson. When am I going home, did Dr. Harmon say?"

Roy took a long look at the patient's chart, then proceeded with his examination. "Well," said the doctor. "I think we will have to keep you a bit longer until we're sure you don't need another transfusion. However, I'll discuss it with Dr. Harmon."

Roy walked toward the door, and Mr. Brimm called him back to introduce him to his wife. Looking at Roy's name, which was printed on his identity badge, Mr. Brimm said to his wife, "This is Dr. McPherson, Dr. Rhoyan McPherson."

Mrs. Brimm stretched out her hand, and Roy shook it.

"He has my middle name," Brimm said jokingly, and with that, Roy excused himself and left the room. He stopped briefly and spoke with doctors at his grandfather's bedside, then plunged himself right into his day without paying any attention to his earlier call on Mr. Brimm.

On Friday, Roy mentioned to Trudy that he was going to call on his mother after he left the hospital but promised to be home for dinner. He headed out to the farm shortly after six o'clock that evening to be sure he arrived after his dad and Rory left for the tournament. His sister was just leaving on her date with Michael Bradford when he turned into the driveway. He waved at her, parked his car, and hurried up to the house. Fiona was sitting in the living room knitting when Roy entered.

"Well, Mom, here I am," he said as he sat down beside her. "Could you tell me what's bothering you and why the urgency?" he continued.

She turned and gave her son a soft hug. Then lifting a cup of tea to her lips, she said, "I am glad you came. I need you to listen to what I have to say. I don't need your judgment, just your understanding." A sudden calmness came over her that almost took her breath away. She paused for a while, then began telling her story.

"When I was eighteen years old, I attended the graduation party of a classmate of mine. He was going away to college while I stayed home to attend a local college. We were very much in love, we danced all evening. The party was held at his parents' home, which was only a few blocks from where we lived. The place got crowded after a while, and we wanted to be alone, so we slipped through the side door into the basement and spent some time making out on an old couch there. When we went back up to the party, I sat for the rest of the evening while he replenished the ice bucket and mixed more Kool-Aid. After the party, I stayed back, along with a few of his buddies, to help with cleaning up. He said he would take me home since it was very late. When we were about to leave, he held my hand and pulled me through the side door, and we ran down to the basement again. He asked if I was all right and wanted to know if I was not going to kiss him once more before he left. I said I was fine, and we kissed and made out again. I was nervous, that was the first time I ever made out with a boy. The next week before he left for college, he called to say good-bye and promised to write often.

"It was late summer when I started college that September. It all went quite well, but at the beginning of fall, I found it difficult to concentrate. I received a letter from him soon after he left home in which he described his dorm and the college and said he was looking forward to coming back home for Thanksgiving. It didn't take long for me to begin feeling ill. I had been irregular before but not for that length of time, so I was distraught because I knew how such a thing would affect my family. Then I wrote to him in October telling him what I had suspected, but he wanted no part of it. In his reply, he urged me to take care of the situation and not let it become a burden on him. He also indicated that it would be best for both of us if his family knew nothing about my condition. I sent him a note saying we must talk it over when he came home for Thanksgiving, but I never heard from him after that. Thanksgiving came, and he did not return. I felt alone and forsaken. I could neither eat nor sleep. Mom and Dad started to notice how frail I had become. I could not go back to college because I was too ill. Mom dragged me off to the doctor who confirmed my fears, which only made things worse at home for me, so I found a way to deal with the daily criticism."

"And how did you do that?" Roy asked quickly.

"Well," said his mother, "I locked myself in my room all day and only came out when Dad went to work and Mom went shopping. One morning, when I was being sick, they entered the room and gave me a good lecture. They said I had to let them know who did this to me because I should not go through it alone. Granddad was especially angry because I did not tell them who the boy was. He withdrew and stopped speaking to me. Your grandma was also furious. Gerald made sure he brought me milk every evening and always fixed a plate of dinner for me. I kept to myself all the time, only leaving my room when no one was around. I was not even seen by a doctor after the initial visit. On Sundays when the family went to church, I got dressed and went for long walks. I knew that they usually gave Aunt Violet a lift home after church, visited her for a while, and have a light lunch before returning home. It was customary for them to leave home at ten a.m. and get back at two p.m., so I had four hours all to myself. My walks sometimes took me past the home of the Brimms, but I never got a chance of seeing him.

"One morning in May about four a.m., I woke with terrible stomach pains. I thought it was the fish stew which Gerald brought for me the night before. I woke him up and told him to get Mother. When she saw my condition, she woke Dad and asked him to take me to the hospital. He called an ambulance instead. When I arrived there, I was taken to the maternity floor. Mother remained in the hallway as I was wheeled into an examining room. She later left when she was told that I would be there for a while. She returned hours later and panicked when she did not see me in the room where she left me, but she was informed at the nurses' station that I was in delivery, and she should sit in the waiting area. However, I later found out that she paced the floor praying silently as she tried to keep calm. Soon after, the doctor appeared to announce that a tiny baby boy was born. Mom waited by the doorway to see you before they took you to the nursery and then followed as I was taken to a room where she sat with me until I fell asleep. Having consulted the doctor, Mother told me that I would be discharged in four days.

"She brought clothes, a blanket, coat, bonnet, and booties for you and looked on while the nurse dressed you. Dad waited in the car for us. He was very happy to see you and nodded affectionately to me as I got into the car. When we arrived home, I went to my room at once to change, have a shower, and wash my hair. On entering, I was quite surprised to see a beautiful little crib and a chest of drawers from Mom and Dad. They were filled with clothes and blankets from Aunt Violet. You slept peacefully in your grandfather's arms until it was time to feed you. Mom cared for both of us during those initial days. After a few weeks, your grandfather bought you a carriage, and I took you for afternoon strolls. It was on one of those afternoons that I met your dad. He knew your grandfather quite well and admired me for a long time, but I did not meet him before then. Six months after, we became friends. He asked me to marry him. I am telling you this, son, because that old man in the hospital, George Brimm, may well be your grandfather."

Roy listened to his mother with rapt attention, his gaze fixed on the floor. Then hearing her last words, he looked up and said, "Who said anything about George Brimm?"

Fiona looked at her son inexplicably. After a long pause, he told her quietly that the man in the hospital was Steven Brimm. Fiona's face revealed her surprise. "Steve?" she asked.

"Yes," said Roy.

"Then he is the one," she said.

"You mean he is my father!" exclaimed Roy.

"Well," Fiona sighed, "unless there is another Steven Brimm out there with a scar on his right hip."

"How did you know it was his right hip? I never mentioned what side the scar was on," Roy questioned.

"I know," said his mother. "The whole school knew. He was on the swim team, he was the fastest swimmer in school. They called him the Lightning Scar."

"I have the same scar," Roy said in a quiet voice, not wanting to meet his mother's gaze.

"Yes," she said. "That's how I knew you were connected."

"That's not all," Roy added. "I also have the same blood type."

There was silence for a while; then Fiona said, "The reason I've told you all this is because you needed to know who your biological father really is. Also, no one else knows this."

"You mean Dad never asked you who my father was?" asked Roy.

"Oh yes!" replied his mother. "But I told him, as far as I am concerned, you have no other father, and he must never ever think of it or ask me that again."

"And he never did?" Roy asked surprised.

"He loves me and respects my wishes," continued Fiona. "No, he never did. When he first met me with you, he thought you were my baby brother, but he quickly realized that you were mine." Fiona's voice quivered as she spoke, "I'm sure he saw the pain in my face and understood my situation, that's why he pursued me until I consented to marry him." Placing an arm around her son, Fiona whispered, "You see, Roy, he loved you so much and wanted to give you so much that he hated the thought of any other father in your life. He just wanted me to stop hurting, and more than anything, he wanted to be there for you." Fiona finished her tea and began putting away her knitting in silence.

Roy stared out the window for a while then, looking back at his mother, asked, "What about Grandma and Grandpa? How did they react to that?"

Placing the basket on the floor, Fiona said with a sigh, "They were relieved.

Your grandpa knew him and was happy that he was interested in me even though I had a child." Then managing a giggle, Fiona said, "You know, most people thought we got married because Sandy fathered you." Then with a grimace, she added in a disgusted way, "I think even the Brimms thought so."

Roy stayed a little longer than he had hoped with his mother. She was upset at having to give him this news. She told him that she loved him dearly and would never have parted with him. "You were conceived by an irresponsible love, but it was an unconditional love for you that brought you into this world and raised you," she murmured as she looked at him through tear-filled eyes.

"Thanks for letting me know about this, Mom," Roy said as he got up to leave. He hugged his mother tightly and kissed her on both cheeks and assured her that she did not have to worry about it anymore. "There is just one thing I would like to know." He paused as he was heading for the door. "I figured out that I was born before you and Dad were married by the date of your anniversary. I just dismissed it as one of those things when Dad satisfied my curiosity by saying, 'We had a jumpstart on our family.' What I would like to know is how you managed to get McPherson on my birth certificate?"

Fiona slumped on a chair; then straightening up, she explained, "I did not give the name of your father before leaving the hospital, so the birth was registered as father unknown. When we got married, Sandy legally adopted you. McPherson is not on your original birth certificate, just on all your other legal documents."

"Oh! Is that so?" Roy frowned. "I never noticed it at all."

"I know," Fiona said, smiling sheepishly. "I took care of that. I made sure that you did not. Not before I had the chance of telling you all about it."

Roy said goodnight, hugged his mother again, and made his way through the front door. A huge love and admiration began swelling up inside him for his dad, Sandy. As he stepped onto the porch, a car pulled up. Rose and her fiancé had returned from the movies. Roy hugged his sister and brother-in-law-to-be, then left. On his way home, he thought about what his mother had said. He had mixed feelings about it all. He knew there was no way he could continue helping Dr. Harmon with his patient. He knew that the conflict of interest would be against medical ethics. He had an increased respect for Sandy and was determined not to let this newfound knowledge interfere with their relationship.

When Roy arrived home, he apologized to his wife for his lateness, washed up, and sat at the dinner table. Trudy was surprised; she thought he must have eaten dinner with his mother since he spent such a long time with her. She subtly tried to find out what happened at the farm, but Roy had no intentions of talking about it. The next morning, he called his mother to inquire if she told his dad about his visit with her, but Fiona had not, and Roy was somewhat relieved to hear it. He wasn't quite sure he was ready to have his bloodline disclosed.

Roy did not call on Mr. Brimm at the hospital after that. He spoke with Dr. Harmon and suggested that he assign another doctor to consult on the case. He gave no reason other than he was extremely busy and may not be in a position to give the required attention. Steven Brimm was subsequently discharged from the hospital, and Roy did not see him any longer.

Weeks passed and Fiona said nothing to her husband about the conversation she had with her son. She felt that it would be better to leave things as they were for the time being and confided her feelings to Roy. She also made him promise not to let Sandy know that he had an encounter with his biological father.

Chapter 9
A Time to Grieve

Life continued as usual for the family. Raymond spent his weekends with his grandmother and accompanied her to the hospital to see his grandpa. Since taking a job in the city, he spent almost all his time away from the farm, and Sandy was grateful that Rory was around to lend a hand with the day-to-day aspects of farming. He also successfully managed the small canning company with a moderate staff while working on plans to make it a big enterprise.

After pushing her past behind her for the better part of her life, Fiona found it once again creeping up to haunt her. Silly thoughts invaded her mind, and she wondered if Steve Brimm may try to contact her or if he ever thought of what happened to the child she was carrying. A knock on the bedroom door brought her back to reality. She looked around to see Sandy standing in the doorway with a basket of fresh fruits.

"You must take this for Elsie when you go to visit your father," he said as he arranged the fruit he had just picked.

Fiona pondered awhile, her eyes transfixed on the basket. Then turning her back to him, she continued fluffing pillows. Managing a faint smile, she told her husband that she had decided to visit the hospital only when he could make the trip with her.

"Why such a somber look? Is everything all right?" he asked.

"Yes." Her reply was quick as she tried to conceal her feelings.

"Then what's this all about?"

"Oh nothing, I just thought it would be nice if you could make some time to go with me, that's all."

Sandy turned away. "I'll put this in the larder, we can take it this weekend."

Fiona smiled at her husband's remarks, and an aura of tranquility embraced her.

Three months after being discharged from the hospital, Steven Brimm returned for some routine checkups. He was slowly walking along the central corridor when he saw Roy.

"Good morning, Dr. McPherson," he said.

Roy looked around and was a bit uneasy to see the man. "Oh hello," he replied. "Where are you headed?"

"Just a checkup," Brimm replied.

"Well, don't let me keep you," Roy said.

"Dr. McPherson, may I ask you a quick question?" Brimm moved closer to Roy.

"What is it?" the doctor said impatiently, checking his watch.

"I've been meaning to ask you this a long time," Steve Brimm continued, "but never got the chance of seeing you before I was discharged. May I ask where you saw a scar like mine?"

Roy paused and looked at the man, surveying his face intently. Then moving away, he said quickly, "I'm sorry, I cannot divulge such information. You must excuse me, I'll be late for my patients." Roy dismissed this meeting with Mr. Brimm and did not mention it to his mother.

The weekend that followed, Roy stopped by his grandmother's to accompany her to the hospital to visit his grandfather. The old man's condition had begun to deteriorate, and the young doctor was quite cautious about breaking this news to his grandmother. It was a cloudy day. He parked his car at the curb in front of the house and ran in to get Elsie. When they came out, the rain had begun to fall, and Roy held an umbrella over the old lady as she got into his car. Just then, someone drove past and beeped his horn while waving at them. Roy never got to see who it was and did not recognize the car. Steve Brimm often drove past the Leighton's residence on his way to visit his mother, she having lived alone since the demise of her husband some years before.

For the next three weeks, Elsie kept a constant vigil at her husband's bedside. She wanted to be present if he should open his eyes. Sadly, however, that day did not come. John Leighton passed away quietly while in a coma.

Elsie was overcome with grief but drew strength from her children and grandchildren who rallied around her. Sandy and Gerald left the hospital to bring the cars around while the family sat quietly in the lobby, their faces twisted in sadness. It was early in the day; they all had a long night and wanted more than anything to see the last of that hospital.

No one noticed the man who walked through the main door and continued through the lobby. He was about to pass them when he noticed Roy and paused. Then recognizing old Mrs. Leighton, he nodded. He touched Roy on his shoulder and whispered, "Doctor, is anything wrong?"

"Just a death in the family," the doctor murmured.

And with that, Steve Brimm continued on his way to keep his appointment. As he reached the revolving doors that led to the clinic, he stopped abruptly as if something had hit him. He looked back at the group and stared a long time at Fiona who had just joined them, bringing a glass of water for her mother. He could not see her face fully because of where she stood. Trying not to look too obvious, he pushed the door and made his way around, entering again, then left with his gaze still fixed on Fiona.

Later that day, he ran into Dr. McPherson again before leaving the hospital. Brimm wasted no time in offering his sympathy and asked who it was that passed away.

"My grandfather," Roy said softly.

"Is that old Mr. Leighton?" Brimm asked. "Is he your grandfather?"

Roy nodded and walked away. He could feel the eyes of the man follow him down the corridor and could not help wondering if that coincidental meeting was not planned.

It was a sad time for the family. Fiona and Aunt Violet stayed with Elsie at her home. Sandy and Gerald made arrangements for the funeral. The little church in Hillcrest was packed to capacity on that day. Everyone came to pay their respects, even Steve Brimm, who none of the family noticed. He was curious after seeing Fiona at the hospital and wanted to attend the funeral for that very reason. At the end of the service, he waited at the foot of the stairs for an opportunity to see Fiona. He approached her just as she was about to enter the car. Stretching out his hand, he offered his sympathy and said her name softly. Fiona looked up when she heard him say, "Remember me? I'm Steve, Steve Brimm."

"Oh!" she said and then thanked him, entered the car, and closed the door.

While they waited for Sandy to join them, Fiona sat quietly with her mother and daughter as the warm April sun shone brightly through the open window. Moving to the other side of the car and bending to give his outstretched hand to Elsie Leighton through the window, Steve Brimm offered his sympathy once more. As he straightened up, his eyes met Fiona's, and he murmured, "Your daughter?" Fiona nodded. Just then, Sandy opened the front door on the passenger side, and Steve Brimm waved as they drove away. Not wanting to appear too obvious, he hurried across the street and around the corner to where his car was parked.

Yes indeed, Mr. Brimm had satisfied his curiosity, and now his conscience bothered him, especially after seeing Sandy. Though just a brief encounter, it was enough to arouse some suspicions in him. When he got home, he went through some old photos of himself, taken when he first joined the company. He was the same height and build as Roy and noticed some resemblance too, or so he thought. He wondered if his mind was playing a silly game with him after all those years. Inane thoughts haunted Brimm for quite some time. He desperately wanted to have some peace of mind, especially before his next appointment at the hospital, should he happen to have another encounter with Dr. McPherson.

Steve Brimm decided that it was time to let his wife know what was bothering him. So one evening after dinner, when they were alone, he told her all about his young life and the son he thought he may have. She was surprised that it took twenty years of marriage for him to tell her of his past. Nevertheless, she was very supportive and offered to help get the information he needed from her contacts at the town's registry.

It took a few weeks for life in its normalcy to prevail again in Fiona's family. Aunt Violet moved in with Elsie just before Fiona returned home. Gerald and Fiona tried their best to encourage their mother to move to the farm, but the old lady would not hear of it. "I belong here, and my memories are here and here I'll stay," they heard her say. Elsie loved spending time on the farm with her daughter and family but did not want to leave her home in Hillcrest. Sandy made sure that Ralphie and Raymond spent each alternate weekend with their grandmother. Roy checked on her most days, and Trudy took her shopping every week.

Midsummer came very quickly, and Meadowbrook Farm became the hub of excitement for family and friends. The wedding of Rose and Michael Bradford was close at hand, and gifts were arriving for the bride and groom from every quarter. Fiona was as nervous as the bride herself. There had not been such a big wedding in the family before. Mayor Bradford insisted on using the ballroom at his golf club for the occasion and reserved several rooms at the Globe Hotel nearby for his family and friends. Fiona constantly checked the arrangements to make sure everything was just perfect. She truly wanted it to be very memorable for her only daughter, although it seemed like the Bradfords had pretty much taken control of most of the planning.

The big day came and went without a hitch; everyone had a great time. Never was there so much hilarity in one place. The couple was not even allowed to leave before the final dance. The next day, Sandy roasted a suckling pig in his backyard, and both families enjoyed a sumptuous farm picnic.

When life settled down and her mother and aunt returned to Hillcrest, Fiona missed having her daughter around the house. There was no one to share a moment with when Sandy and Rory went bowling or played pool. Although they spoke on the phone daily, she missed her daughter's cold feet huddled next to hers under the covers when they sat in front of the fireplace crocheting. Sandy and Fiona visited Elsie most weekends. They did not give up trying to get her to change her mind about going to live with them. Aunt Violet was in total agreement, but her sister would not hear of it. Although Fiona did not discuss the presence of Steve Brimm at the funeral, she knew it was just a matter of time when her mother may well mention it.

New developments were taking place back at the farm. Rory had completed all his plans to expand the cottage industry and introduce his mother's recipes for homemade jams and jellies to a wider population. They were going to tear down the old barn, which sat on a large piece of land behind the house, and put up a modern factory. Both Rory and his father were quite enthused about the project and hoped to have construction started before the winter. Rory had been dating his sister's best friend and maid of honor since the wedding and was more than thrilled when she offered to have her grandfather, a retired architect, involved in the plans for the building.

That year, the family decided to spend Thanksgiving in Hillcrest with Grandma Leighton. They wanted it to be special and to capture some of the magic of the holidays that was there years before. This was the first holiday without their grandfather, and it had been several years since they all came together in Hillcrest for Thanksgiving.

The weather was mild that fall. Trees took time to array themselves in colorful attire. It was late November, and the foliage had just begun to fall. With a small suitcase and a crate in which a large live turkey sat, Fiona started out on her journey to spend a few days with her mother before the rest of the family descended upon the Leighton house. Arriving a few days early would afford her the advantage of a head start with all the necessary preparations.

Gerald and his family arrived the evening before Thanksgiving and stayed with Roy. The rest of the family began trickling in early that morning, and by noon, Elsie's house became a home once more. Everyone chipped in and helped in any way they could. The old lady was overjoyed to have her children, grandchildren, and great-grandchild all together in Hillcrest for the holiday. Her sister, Violet, was especially pleased since she had not been moving around much and missed out on most family gatherings.

Chapter 10
The Letter

Aflu epidemic accompanied the cold winter months that followed the beginning of another year. Emergency rooms, clinics, and doctors' offices were overrun with patients. Roy had just seen his last patient for the day. He called his wife to let her know he would be home shortly.

"Take your time," she said lightheartedly. "I'm sure something would turn up as it always does."

"No, I don't think so, I've had it for today. Someone else would have to take over if necessary," replied Roy.

He hung up the phone; took off his white coat; grabbed his hat, scarf, and coat from a nearby closet; and then came a knock on the door. *Who could that be?* he wondered. *The staff should still be out there. Why would they let anyone in without buzzing him first?* Thinking it may be the cleaners since it was already very late, Roy reached for the door. He opened it to find Steven Brimm standing there, looking much thinner than he did a year ago.

"Mr. Brimm!" Roy sounded as surprised as he looked. "Did you have an appointment? How did you get in?"

"Eh, well, I noticed that no one was at the front desk, so I just thought I could deliver this personally," Brimm said as he held out his hand with an envelope in it.

"What can I do for you?" Roy asked.

The man shifted nervously from one foot to the other. "Kindly deliver this letter to your mother for me, and please tell her I am truly sorry. I would have posted it, but I do not have her address. I shall be very grateful if you will hand it over to her for me."

Roy took the letter from Steve Brimm, nodded approvingly, then slowly backed away from the opened door. The middle-aged man shook the doctor's hand tightly, thanked him, and left. Roy locked the letter in the top drawer of his desk and quickly left the office, slipping through the back entrance. On the way home, he thought about the letter and wondered why Steve Brimm would be sorry about the passing of his grandfather almost a year after. He thought it very strange.

"As usual, Trudy was right," he muttered to himself as he pulled into the driveway. He was glad that this meeting with Steve Brimm did not take up too much of his time. Roy called his mother the next day to let her know about the letter. He said he would hand it over to her that weekend when she came into town.

Fiona was very curious. "Read it to me on the phone," she told him.

"I don't think I should," he said. "Surely it can wait."

She felt embarrassed about her impatience. "Yes, it could," she assured her son.

The weekend seemed to take longer than ever to arrive. Fiona could not wait to read the letter that Roy left for her. He had placed it in an antique vase on top of the china cabinet when he visited his grandmother earlier that day. She found a quiet moment to slip into the laundry room where she stood with her back to the door and began to read.

> *Dear Fiona,*
>
> *I'm so sorry for everything that happened when we were so young. I did not realize that you had such a big son until I saw you with Dr. McPherson when your father passed away last year. I had the pleasure of meeting him during my hospitalization but did not know he was your son at the time. Seeing you at the funeral brought many memories to mind. I decided to take the liberty of finding out Dr. McPherson's date of birth and was not surprised that he was born exactly nine months after I left for college. The fact that he has my middle name "Rhoyan." which is in itself unusual, prompted me to do so. I hope you will forgive me for this. I am glad to know that you are happy and have such a wonderful family. I am also married and have two daughters. I would very much like to know if I have a son and if he has a scar*

*on his hip. I shall be grateful if you will answer this question for
me. I would like to introduce myself to him if that is acceptable
to you. Kindly let me have your answer by return mail to the
above address.*

Sincerely,
Steven Brimm

Fiona read the letter once more, then picked up the laundry, and went
upstairs without mentioning anything about it to her mother or aunt. A
surge of anger overcame her, but that slowly gave way to pity as she tried
desperately to control her emotions. She knew she had to let Sandy know
about this man. She could no longer put off revealing his identity. *Why did
he want to know?* she questioned herself. He seemed to be imposing, and she
hated it. Moreover, she hated herself for giving in to her childish fantasy by
naming her son Rhoyan. When her parents questioned her about the name,
she simply told them he will be called Roy. It was a silly thing to do, but she
was not going to bother about that extraordinary name she loved so much
for her son.

When Fiona returned home, she gave Sandy the letter to read. He
already knew the circumstances surrounding the birth of Roy, and now that
the letter revealed the identity of the biological father of his son, he was able
to let go of secret suspicions. He stared at the paper for a long time, then
gave it back to Fiona. He told her that he was fine with whatever decision
she and Roy made concerning the man. He said he was relieved to have that
information after years of speculating but did not care for this intrusion
upon his family.

After consulting her son, Fiona replied to Steven Brimm. Putting pen
to paper brought back bitter memories of the last letter she wrote to him
more than thirty years ago. That was all behind her now. She was proud to
be the mother of such a brilliant young man. She knew that Steve was the
loser, and that brought on a selfish arrogance, something Fiona did not care
to hide in her reply that read,

Dear Steve Brimm,
    *I received your letter with mixed emotions. I half expected
it many years ago. I had a feeling that one day, you will meet
my son, Dr. McPherson. He is the product of our young love
and does have a scar on his hip to prove it. However, he also*

63

*has a very loving and caring father who raised him as his own
from the time he was seven months old and whom he thinks the
world of. You may introduce yourself to him if you wish. I will
tell him to expect it. He already knows who you are. My son is
a fine gentleman. I trust you will respect his privacy and that of
my family as well.*

(Sgd.) *Fiona McPherson*

After having her husband's opinion of the reply, she mailed it. They both
hoped that there would be no more intrusion of this sort into their lives and
felt confident that Roy would be able to handle whatever situation arose with
respect to his acknowledgment of the man Steven Brimm.

One month after receiving Fiona's reply, Steve made an appointment to
see Roy. He requested the very last appointment time in the doctor's schedule
for the day and made sure he arrived on time. When his chart was placed
on the doctor's desk, Roy looked at it briefly, then closed the file, and waited
for the patient. He wondered what the man's intent was since treatment of
him was not an option. The door opened slowly, and Mr. Brimm made his
appearance.

Before Roy could say anything, the man said quickly, "I'm not here as
a patient. This is the only way I felt I had a chance of speaking with you
in private. I promise not to take up too much of your valuable time. I just
wanted to meet you again and introduce myself properly."

"Please have a seat," Roy said, pointing to a chair on the other side of
his desk.

Steve thanked him and continued speaking as he sat. "I am glad to have
the opportunity of knowing you," he said. "I don't want you to feel obligated
in any way. I am sorry for my youthful decision that has placed us in such an
awkward situation. If ever you need any medical information concerning my
family history, you would find it in my medical records," he told Roy. "Please
feel free to ask me whatever you like."

Brimm shifted nervously in his chair. Roy looked at the man who sat
across the desk from him. He was thin and drawn and looked much older
than he really was. He didn't know what to say to him, and then with a flip
of the chart, he asked, "How is your health?"

Steve cleared his throat, then answered, "Well, I am doing fine so far.
How are you coping with the demands of Hillcrest Hospital?"

"Good, good," Roy replied.

Steve looked at a photo on the desk and asked, "Is this your family?"

"Yes, my wife and son."

"You have a beautiful wife and what a handsome boy. I do hope I can meet him someday."

Roy was silent for a while. Then looking at the photograph, he said, "Maybe you could."

Steve fumbled in his pocket, then brought out a photo, and handed it to Roy. "These are my daughters. Maybe one day you will meet them also."

Roy looked at the photo, then handed it back, saying, "Very lovely girls."

"Will leave you now," Brimm said as he rose to his feet, pushed back the chair, and stretched out his hand.

Roy got up and shook the man's hand. His grip was firm. Steve placed another hand over Roy's and held on tightly. He looked into his eyes and said, "I'm glad I got to know you before it's too late. I'll always be grateful for this opportunity." He then smiled, and letting go of Roy's hand, he turned to the door. "It was nice seeing you."

Roy said, "Do take good care of yourself."

Steve turned and looked back at the photograph on the desk, and Roy felt a sudden compulsion to compromise. As he followed him to the door, he said, "We will be accompanying my grandmother to a family service next Sunday at her church. If you could make it, we will meet in the foyer after. But I must warn you, the meeting would only be a brief one."

"Thanks," Steve grinned. "As long as I get to see and touch my grandson."

There was a hint of excitement in his tone; then he opened the door, said good evening, and left, closing it gently behind him.

Roy sat at his desk, examining the chart in front of him, and wondered why fate brought him into contact with this man whom he could not think of as a father or had any feelings for. They had nothing in common apart from a scar and the same bloodline. He felt a bit of pity for him but was determined not to let it prevail in his life.

Family Sunday was always a fun day at their local church. Roy had pleasant memories of many such days spent with his grandparents as a little boy. There were loads of refreshments and Bible trivia for adults and kids alike. After the service, Roy asked his grandmother if she wanted to go to the undercroft of the church for refreshments.

"Don't forget that Mom is expecting me to take you old girls out to the farm for lunch," he quickly added.

Aunt Violet's eyes lit up. "We much prefer going to lunch," she said without hesitation as she reached for her walker.

Trudy helped Aunt Violet to her feet while Roy held his son in his arms. Elsie Leighton nodded approvingly and got up, making her way out of the church with her sister while pausing to greet old friends along the way. On reaching the foyer, Roy looked around for Steve Brimm with a quick glance. Not making a connection, he headed for the door to see if the man was outside and told Trudy to stay with the old ladies while he got the car. Just then, he heard a voice behind him say, "Good morning, Mrs. Leighton."

Roy looked around to see Steve Brimm standing there. His grandmother smiled and nodded.

"Oh hello," Roy said. "This is my Aunt Violet and my wife, Trudy, and this is our son. You do remember Mr. Brimm from Grandpa's funeral, don't you, Grandma?"

Elsie Leighton nodded again and said hello. After shaking hands with everyone, Steve turned his attention to the toddler who had one hand around his father's neck while the other hand was up to his face as he sucked on his thumb.

"What a cute little boy you are, do you have a name?" he said as he pulled the child's cheek.

"Tell the gentleman your name," Roy prompted his son, pulling the finger out of his mouth. "Say Rickey!"

The child gazed at Steve, then slowly buried his head in his father's shoulder.

"Well, I'll go get the car now," Roy said as he turned and moved closer to the door. "Good day again," he said to Steve Brimm and shook his hand. "Say good-bye," he told the child.

Steve held the boy's hand and kissed it, then followed Roy through the door to the parking lot. He then waved and headed in the opposite direction. Roy pulled his car up to the front of the church where the others waited for him. That was the last time Roy saw Steven Brimm.

Fiona listened with rapt attention as her son related his meeting with Steve. They found some quiet time together after lunch that day when the old ladies rested. While Trudy did the dishes and Sandy was occupied with his grandson, Fiona decided to escort her son to see the new factory building. Once inside, Roy told his mother about the man she did not know. He thanked her for telling him about the boy she knew and assured her that he loved his dad and would not trade him for the world, especially not for the man whose bloodline he shared.

"I wonder where all this would lead," Fiona murmured as the two made their way back to the house.

"I don't know, and I don't intend to give it another thought," Roy replied. "I just hope you would do the same, Mom. What's done is done. We are who we are now, and no one can change or divide us. I must confess that I am flooded with pity for this man. His eyes show so much pain, but that has little to do with me and everything to do with him. I am glad it all came out now so I can put it behind me." Roy sounded a little unsure.

"I hope you can do so," his mother said firmly as she squeezed his hand. "I hope you can forgive me and your father for keeping this from you for so long."

They entered the house to find Sandy comfortably seated in the rocking chair with his grandson sleeping on his lap. The old ladies were still napping, and Trudy had the kitchen all tidied up and was preparing the table for coffee and cake. Rory arrived home just before they left. He was overjoyed to see his grandmother and great-aunt. Elsie hugged her grandson tightly and scolded him for not coming to see her more often. "I see your brothers all the time, but I seldom see you," she said, pulling his ear.

Rory smiled, his brown eyes twinkling as he said, "The farm, Grandma, the farm keeps me quite busy, and I rarely get into Hillcrest, but I promise to surprise you soon."

Elsie glanced at her daughter, exclaiming, "Something is brewing! Isn't it? Is another wedding in the air?"

Fiona smiled and turned to Rory in reply. "Ask him, don't ask me."

Rory laughed loudly, and a blush came over his handsome face. He hugged his grandmother and great-aunt once more, then hurried into the kitchen to fix himself a plate. Roy followed his brother.

"What's this I'm hearing?" he asked.

"Well, I'm thinking of settling down," Rory replied.

"Wow!" Roy exclaimed. "Is it pretty Ms. Maid-of-Honor?"

Rory smiled again and nodded. "You'll be the first to know, chum," he told his brother.

Roy and Rory have always been very close. The same empty feeling that came over Rory when his brother announced his engagement to Trudy years before had begun to creep over Roy.

"I'll be waiting," he said. "Don't let me keep you from your dinner. Call me." And with that, he left the kitchen.

Everyone was on the porch, chatting and waiting for Roy.

"Come again soon!" Fiona shouted as they drove off into the setting sun of a warm Sunday afternoon.

Chapter 11
The Revelation

Days, weeks, and months flew by. Fiona was busy knitting blankets and booties for Rose's first baby when Rory announced that he was going to be engaged. Two months after his engagement party, her daughter-in-law Trudy announced that she was expecting their second child. Everything seemed to happen all at once. Rose gave birth to a beautiful baby girl on her wedding anniversary. *What a lovely gift from God,* Fiona thought. Her family was growing, everyone was doing well, and she had everything to be thankful for, including finally being able to reconcile her past.

Mondays were always very busy days at hospital and clinics alike. Roy had just seen the last of his patients and decided to go home for an early dinner—to spend the evening with his family and tuck his son in bed, something he did not get to do very often. Trudy was in her third trimester and experienced increased tiredness. She was happy to have her husband home much earlier than usual on a Monday. As they sat at the table, Roy's eyes stared at the envelope propped up beside the centerpiece. It was boldly written "Private & Confidential" and addressed to him.

"What's this?" he questioned.

"I don't know, but surely it can wait until after dinner."

Roy pretended to be unconcerned about the letter but noticed it came from a law firm and was curious about its contents. He never had any reasons for malpractice. *What if the hospital was involved in anything I knew nothing about?* he thought as he finished his meal. Lifting his glass to his mouth, he took several quick gulps of water, sat back in his chair, then reached for the letter. Trudy also became very curious at that point; her eyes were focused on her husband as he tore open the envelope and began reading silently. She watched his expression go from blank stare to knitted brows. When he was finished, he kept looking at the two-page letter as if it were written in a foreign language.

"What's wrong?" she asked. Roy was pensive. "Is it about the hospital?"

Roy shook his head, then exclaimed, "I can't believe this!"

"What?" she asked again.

Roy gave a long sigh and then said softly, "He died, Mr. Brimm is dead. He named me in his will. Why would he do that? What am I going to do with his company?"

"What company?" Trudy inquired.

"Well, it looks as though he owned an engineering firm of some sort," Roy continued. "They want me to contact them to set up an appointment to hand over the necessary papers and advised that I assign a personal attorney to take care of any other legal matters in this regard."

"Who wants this?" Trudy asked.

"The law firm that sent me this letter," he said irritably, kicking back his chair as he stood up. "Let me help you with these dishes," he mumbled as he placed the letter on the table.

Trudy picked it up and read it. "You must make the appointment," she said. "That is the only way you would know what this entails and why you were given this honor."

"I know why I was given this honor, someday I will tell you all about it. It is obvious that he felt guilty about me," Roy told his wife. "But I didn't know he felt that guilty. What would his family think?" Roy sounded worried. "No!" he said. "I don't need this, I won't let this happen. Before I make an appointment, I will meet with Mrs. Brimm. I have to know where she stands in all this. I have to let her know that I had nothing to do with it and have no intentions of impinging on their inheritance." He was firm as he spoke, "I will get on this right away. The quicker it is out of my hands, the better it will be for all concerned."

Roy did not sleep well at all that night. He felt quite annoyed that this man who he hardly knew found a way to drag him into his affairs. He was determined not to be a part of this game. The next morning, he locked the letter in his desk drawer and left for the hospital to make his early rounds. He had his receptionist connect him to Mrs. Brimm in the early afternoon. She seemed pleased to hear from him and agreed to have him call on her that Friday evening. Roy did not tell his mother about the inheritance or the passing of Steve Brimm. He felt that he could solve whatever problems arose as a result of this and forbade Trudy from mentioning any of it to the family.

Friday evening couldn't have come quicker for Roy. He arrived home at six, picked up the letter, and left for the Brimm residence. He was impressed but not surprised at the size of the house that appeared at the end of a long driveway. He parked the car and was greeted at the door by a familiar face, one he had seen before at the hospital. An exchange of pleasantries ended with Roy's condolence and an apology for not knowing about the demise of Mrs. Brimm's husband. He was surprised to learn that the middle-aged lady had already been widowed for two months. She led him to a quiet room, which was fitted with bookshelves on every wall. There was a coffee table in the middle with a tray of hors d'oeuvres, a silver coffee set, and two crystal coffee mugs. A leather sofa set surrounded the table. Mrs. Brimm removed a pillow from an armchair and beckoned Roy to sit. She sat opposite him and asked if he preferred to have a cool drink or coffee. Roy thanked her but declined the offer. He got right to the point and told her that he came to discuss the letter that he received from her attorneys.

"Before you go any further," Mrs. Brimm said, "let me tell you the reason for that letter. Your father was very happy to learn that he had a son, his own flesh and blood,—an heir so to speak. He was grieved to know that you went through life not knowing him, or he not knowing about you. He told me how proud he was to finally make your acquaintance and to see the successful young man you have become. Steven always wanted a child of his own, his final days were fulfilled." She paused.

Roy looked at her intently, then asked, "You do have children, don't you?"

"Oh yes, two girls," she said. "And from the sound in the hallway, you should get to meet them right away."

She barely finished speaking when a dark-eyed, chubby-cheeked teenager peeped into the room.

"This is Dr. McPherson," her mother said, introducing Roy. "And this is my young daughter Jane."

"Nice to know you, Jane," Roy said as he rose to his feet.

The girl stretched out her hand and shook Roy's. "Same here," was her reply.

"Where is Cara?" her mother asked.

"Oh! She will be down in a while. Her friends will come over for a game of scrabble," the young teen said as she sauntered out of the room.

"Sweet child, how old is she?" Roy asked politely.

"Fifteen going on thirty," Mrs. Brimm answered smiling. "Sorry about the interruption. I was telling you what prompted your father to rethink his will." She continued, "My husband lost his only sibling, a younger brother, many years ago in an accident. He was in his twenties. When his father passed on several years after, the firm was left to Steven and his cousin who only inherited a very small share. When he became ill, Steven knew he had to make a serious decision about the firm. I agreed to step in and hire an executive director to run things. His cousin also works for the firm, but Steven felt he was not worthy of his inheritance."

The doorbell rang interrupting the conversation again. Jane ran to the door while screaming at the top of her voice for her sister to come downstairs.

"Be quiet!" their mother urged. Just then, Cara appeared and signaled her mother's attention. She wanted her to know that the girls will be playing their games upstairs instead.

"This is Dr. McPherson, Cara," Mrs. Brimm told her daughter.

"Goodnight, Doctor," she responded. "Can I get you anything, Mom?" she said, moving closer, giving an outstretched hand to Roy who rose once more to his feet to acknowledge the girl. When she turned to leave the room, Roy noticed that she dragged her left foot. When she was out of the room, he asked her mother if she had an injury.

"No," she replied. "She was born that way. When we got her, she was four years old and had a slight limp. But as she grew, we noticed it had become increasingly difficult for her to walk. We took her to several doctors, but they all said she was born with a deformity that should have been corrected at birth."

"So she is adopted?" Roy asked.

"Yes, they both are, they are sisters. Cara was four and Jane two months old when they came to live with us." Mrs. Brimm noticed the look of surprise on Roy's face, so she continued, "Their father was my husband's best friend. When he joined the navy after they left college, he made Steven promise that if anything should happen to him and he had a family, he would like Steven to be there for them. Likewise, my husband made Carl promise the same thing. They were inseparable from the time they started college together. When we got married, Carl was Steven's best man, and five years later, Steven did the same for Carl. We spent many holidays together, and when Carl died in a boating accident on the French Riviera, Steven took care of his wife, Lena, and daughter, Cara. Lena was three months pregnant at the time, and the shock of her husband's death compromised her weak heart. She wrote to us months later, just before she gave birth, to thank Steven for all his help and asked us to adopt her children if anything should happen to her. Well, she did not survive the birth of Jane. She probably knew she would not and had everything in place for the adoption to go smoothly."

Roy listened intently; he had a lot of questions but refrained from being too inquisitive. "When was she last seen by a specialist?" he asked finally.

"That was some years ago. She was ten years old and had such a painful experience with therapy that she has refused to see any more doctors," the girl's mother recounted.

"Science has advanced over the last ten years. Maybe she could benefit from surgery," Roy advised, but Mrs. Brimm merely shook her head and shrugged her shoulders. It seemed she was uncertain at that point of what action she could take to help this child who appeared to be comfortable with her handicap.

"I'm sorry for rambling on," she said. "Shall we get back to the matter at hand?"

Roy agreed and took charge of the conversation. "I was about to say . . ." He looked at the lady as he held out the letter he pulled from his jacket pocket. "I came to discuss this with you, I really don't want the inheritance. This should go to your daughters." Roy tried not to sound agitated.

"Oh! But they too have a fair inheritance," she insisted. "Your father wanted this to pass on to you, and I can assure you that I will not go against his wishes. You don't understand what this meant to him. I urge you to think it through and let me have your decision in two weeks before the board meets. Please, promise me that at least."

Roy felt helpless; although he had no intentions of accepting the inheritance, he thought it better to let the matter rest for a while. "It's getting late, I'd better be going now," he said. "I promise to think it through and call you in a few days."

Roy thanked Mrs. Brimm for her hospitality as she escorted him to the door. Before he left, she asked him if he had any suggestions regarding her daughter's medical situation. He said he could try to get her an appointment with a well-known orthopedic surgeon in New York who specialized in reconstructive surgery. She thanked him and said she would look forward to it.

Trudy was already in bed by the time Roy returned home. Not wanting to disturb her, he fixed himself a plate and sat at the kitchen table, wondering why his life was taking such turns. He needed sound advice—the kind that he got from his father, Sandy, but it was already too late to be calling. So he waited until the morning to phone and to ask his father and mother if they could come to Hillcrest. Roy was on call at the hospital that weekend and could not make it out to the farm. Fiona got anxious; she dropped all her chores for the day and started preparing for them to leave right away. She knew it had to be a matter of great importance for her son to send for them.

It was early Saturday afternoon when Sandy's pickup pulled into the driveway. Fiona had packed a large basket of fruits and vegetables for Trudy and Elsie and went straight to the kitchen to divide it between them. Sandy looked at his son, their eyes met for a long time, and Roy simply nodded in quiet acknowledgment of his father, a tired look on his face from a sleepless night. Breaking the silence, he asked that they gather in the family room to discuss the matter.

"What's troubling you, son?" Sandy asked.

Fiona left Trudy to sort out the produce and joined her husband and son in the family room. Roy felt embarrassed; however, he pulled himself together and spoke as calmly as he could. He started by showing the letter to his parents and then told them all about his meeting with Mrs. Brimm.

"When did he die?" Fiona asked.

"Two months ago," was Roy's calm reply.

She then asked about Steve Brimm's children. Roy explained that they were adopted. A wave of distrust and fear must have consumed her at that point, causing her to butt in callously. "You have nothing to do with that man's affairs. You are neither his son nor heir, it would be wise to disclaim all this. Who knows what trouble it may bring?" Fiona got up and left the room, feeling ashamed about her outburst of anger.

Sandy asked his son how he felt about accepting such a large inheritance. Roy said he did not think it was right for him and preferred not to acknowledge any family ties with others who he knew nothing about.

"Are you his only biological child?" Sandy asked. "I think you need to know if there are any other siblings who may come out of the woodwork and challenge you for this."

"I don't need to know," Roy protested. "I will have no part of it, so I don't need to know."

"Listen, son," Sandy spoke calmly but firmly. "You need to be sure, you need to speak to Mrs. Brimm again and tell her of this concern."

"Why?" Roy asked. "She will think that I'm interested in the inheritance."

"Never mind that," Sandy argued. "You need to know, and I would like to know as well."

Roy was silent; he valued his father's advice. They sat together in quiet contemplation, Sandy poring over the letter once more.

"I will call her right away," Roy said softly as he reached for the phone.

When the middle-aged widow heard Roy's voice on the line, she greeted him with surprise. "Glad to be hearing from you so soon," she said.

Roy explained that he was calling with a concern about the possibility of other offsprings Steven Brimm might have.

"There are no other heirs apart from my two daughters," Mrs. Brimm said. "I am certain of that."

"How can you be so sure?" Roy asked. "He didn't find out about me until a few years ago."

"Don't worry," she insisted. "Steven had a bad case of mumps at the age of nineteen soon after a hiking trip with friends from college. He did not know it then, but after we got married and it took so long for us to have a child, we both got tested. The results revealed that my husband could not have children. It was hard for both of us at first, but as time went by and we got the girls, it didn't matter anymore. When he found out about you, he was so happy but agonized over the fact that you were never going to be his son. Nevertheless, he wanted to meet you and was grateful for the opportunity of meeting his grandson before he passed. When Steven became very ill and had to make a decision concerning the firm, he told me that he wanted to leave it to you because you are his rightful heir. He only needed my approval, which was the easy part. I shared my husband's agony over this for several years since it was obvious that he would not get to marry off his daughters and so did not know who would be taking control of the firm when they got older. He felt that fate brought you two together, and you were meant to have shares in the firm also. The hard part is convincing you to accept it."

He thanked her for the information and said he would think about it.

Sandy and Fiona listened as Roy recounted his conversation with Mrs. Brimm after hanging up the phone. Fiona was silent, but Sandy encouraged his son to make a firm decision concerning the inheritance since he was the only other heir apart from Brimm's two daughters. He advised him to think about his own children who stood to be heirs as well and how they would feel about his decision when they were old enough to benefit from it.

"He owed you this," Sandy told Roy. "Even if you don't need it, you have every right to accept it. The man stepped out on a limb to name you as his heir despite the fact that legally you are not his son."

"What would you do?" Roy inquired of his father.

"Pass it on to your children, set up a trust for them, and leave the affairs of the company to Mrs. Brimm and the board of directors."

Roy agreed that Sandy's suggestion was a good alternative and decided to look into the possibility of putting it into effect. He valued his father's advice and knew he needed to look past the circumstances of his birth and think about his children who were also blood relatives of Steven Brimm.

Fiona made no contribution to the conversation; she merely listened in silence and was deep in thought. That evening after an early dinner, she and Sandy called on her mother briefly before returning to the farm. Elsie and Aunt Violet were surprised to see them and questioned their being in Hillcrest for the day. Fiona only said they had visited Roy and Trudy to deliver some produce from the farm. The old ladies knew nothing about the connection of Roy to Steve Brimm, and Fiona wanted to keep it that way for the moment.

After his parents left, Roy felt a whole lot better; he was much more relaxed as he discussed his father's advice with Trudy concerning their children's birthright and his connection to the man Steven Brimm. Although she shared Sandy's opinion, Trudy told her husband that she would be happy with whatever decision he made. Roy decided to postpone responding to Mrs. Brimm and her attorneys since he had a time limit of two weeks and therefore shelved the matter for a while.

In the week that followed, he contacted Dr. Burrows and obtained an early appointment for Cara. He had his office call Mrs. Brimm with the date and details for the consultation, and having done so, he was able to put the matter out of his thoughts. Nevertheless, on occasion, he wondered about the reaction from Brimm's relatives who might learn about him and want to meet him. He even thought about old Mrs. Brimm, Steve's mother. Her daughter-in-law did not mention her at all. Was she still alive? And if so, did she know about him too? She would have to be as old as his Grandmother Elsie. Pushing all these thoughts aside, the young doctor immersed himself in his work and tried not to pay any attention to the fortune that was bequeathed to him.

His mother was not that open-minded; she had a hard time dealing with the matter and agonized over her fear that her son could face some embarrassment in light of all the attention that may come his way should he act as the senior executive in a multimillion-dollar company. She wondered how she was going to explain to her other children that Roy was not their father's biological child. It was imminent now that they had to be told; after all, they were adults. As her mind raced for answers, Fiona thought that she had better not jump the gun but rather wait and see what her son's decision was before trying to explain his sudden fortune.

It had been two weeks since she and Sandy visited Hillcrest to discuss the matter with their son, and she remembered his promise to get back in touch with the firm's attorneys at that time. She desperately wanted to know if he took his father's advice to pass on the inheritance to his children or if he was willing to be a major part of the Brimm enterprise. Fiona did not want to come off as intrusive, so she called her son, pretending to remind him that it had been two weeks since their visit. Roy was not at all surprised to hear from his mother that evening. He told her that he had made a few decisions and was going to meet with Mrs. Brimm to discuss placing a small portion of the shares into a trust for his children and cashing in on the greater part.

"What!" Fiona exclaimed in a burst of emotion.

"Well, Mom, I can't explain it in detail now, but the hospital needs a new wing, and I was thinking that I can help them get it," Roy said calmly.

"Oh, I see." Fiona was cautious as she spoke. There was a lot more she wanted to say but decided it was not the time to do so. Before ending the conversation, she inquired about Trudy. Roy told her it was just a matter of weeks until she would have a new grandson. That was definitely music to her ears, but she could not keep herself from thinking how one gesture from someone she loved so long ago would have an effect on that tiny life.

Sandy was proud of his son's decision when he was told about it; however, he noticed the concern on his wife's face. But before he could find out what bothered her so deeply, she merely turned away as she murmured, "How would he explain coming into all that money?"

"Leave him alone," Sandy warned her. "He knows what he is doing and will certainly get the best legal advice."

Nevertheless, Fiona had an uneasy feeling about the whole affair. Was she letting her past determine her son's future? It all seemed so complicated to her. She felt that Steven Brimm was slowly claiming and controlling her son from the grave, but it was only Fiona who thought so. Both Roy and

Sandy shared the view that Brimm suffered remorse and deeply wanted to compensate for turning his back on her when she needed him and for not bothering to find out what had happened to the child she carried. He knew he let his only child and heir slip through his fingers and truly regretted it. Roy felt some pity for the man, but he was not about to be a part of his family or take an interest in their affairs. In fact, he was somewhat relieved to have Sandy as his father and grateful for the opportunity of growing up in a normal family.

The next morning, Roy called Mrs. Brimm to let her know that he was seeking an appointment with the firm's attorneys and requested her presence. At that meeting, he revealed the plan he had for his shares in the firm and was able to obtain the value for the portion he wanted to dispose of. Mrs. Brimm was surprised and a bit disappointed that he saw the need to cash in at the very beginning. Roy did not reveal to any of them the reason for this decision; however, she was satisfied to know that he honored her husband's dying wish by accepting the inheritance and informed him that company policy dictated that shares could only be bought and sold within the family. She further pointed out that she was willing to buy the shares he wanted to dispose of for a reasonable price. After sorting out all legal matters pertaining to the transfer of shares from Steven Brimm to Dr. Roy McPherson as the will stated, the young doctor was then summoned to the next board meeting as a senior partner in the company. Since it was crucial that he knew how many of the company's shares he would have to sell to make his dream of a new hospital wing a reality, Roy wasted no time in finding out from competent authorities how much money was needed for a project of that magnitude. He particularly wanted to have this information before he attended his first board meeting, which was scheduled to take place in a matter of weeks. That meant he would be in a better position to let them know what portion of his shares were up for sale so that early arrangements could be made for transfer of the remainder to a trust for his children.

Sundays were always very relaxing days for Roy and his family—visiting his parents at the farm, having lunch with Trudy's relatives, or this time, like so many others, escorting Grandma Elsie and Aunt Violet to church and enjoying a good old-fashioned home-cooked meal. Elsie Leighton was certainly not as active as she used to be and seldom displayed her culinary skills anymore. However, she enjoyed making an effort for her grandchildren and looked forward to those days when she got the opportunity of entertaining her grandson Roy and his family after Sunday service.

When they returned home, Roy and Trudy lounged in the family room while their young son played nearby. Trudy was overcome by exhaustion and quickly fell asleep, her head nestled on Roy's chest while her slightly swollen outstretched legs rested heavily on the sofa. Roy's mind drifted to the farm and his brother Rory who was to be wed in a matter of a few months. He had been so preoccupied with his own circumstance that he almost forgot he was to be his brother's best man. Stretching out his arm, he reached for the phone and called Rory. The two chatted for a while, and Roy promised to spend the next weekend at the farm if Trudy could make the trip. It was obvious to him that neither of his parents discussed his inheritance with any of his siblings, and he did not feel comfortable to do so. He hung up the phone and rubbed his forehead as if trying to remove any uncertainty.

While he chatted with Rory, he failed to observe the toy box and an array of Lego blocks strewn over the floor. His little son played quietly in a corner of the room, and Roy felt a bit guilty leaving him all by himself while his mother slept and he chatted on the phone. Calling the boy to him, Roy leaned forward to see what he was doing. The structure that rose two feet in the air seemed strangely familiar, so he pulled up a few cushions for his wife and slipped out of the sofa to have a closer look at what fascinated the child. The little boy continued building while his father watched in amazement. He remembered giving him the Lego set for his birthday months before but never had the chance of showing him how to use it. The boy ran back and forth to the toy box looking for the perfect pieces to complete his building and affixing the odd pieces in a pile at the side. When he was finished, he looked up at his father and said, "Look, my barn." Roy knelt on the floor next to his son and looked at the structure. He was astonished at the work of his three-year-old and noticed how closely it resembled the barn at the farm. He pointed to the pile of odd pieces on the floor next to it and asked the child what it represented. "Hay," was his answer. Roy hugged his son for the first time since his birth. He was overcome with so much emotion that he just let the tears flow. It was quite obvious that the skill to produce such a perfect piece without any help or prior knowledge had to be inherited, and for the first time, Roy thought of the connection between his son and the line of architectural engineers he came from.

Chapter 12
An Enemy Within

The day for the board meeting seemed to have arrived much earlier than the doctor anticipated. He had put in extra hours at the clinic in order to get off that afternoon but still felt a bit rushed as he headed over to the city office of the Brimm firm to meet with members of its executive board. After he was ushered into a comfortable conference room, Mrs. Brimm wasted no time in introducing Roy to the associates as the senior shareholder of the firm. Everyone was polite and congratulated him. However, as the meeting progressed, he noticed that the man who was introduced as Steven Brimm's cousin sat next to Mrs. Brimm and whispered continuously in her ear. She appeared uncomfortable with him, but the other four members paid no attention to the man named Jacob Grazi. When the meeting ended, he bent over to Roy and asked him to share a moment with him in his office. The doctor was happy to oblige and followed Grazi down a narrow hallway through large glass doors that opened to an office filled with sports memorabilia. The man got right to the point in questioning Roy about his relationship to his cousin Steven Brimm and offered to buy all the shares he had inherited. He went as far as to say that his cousin was not competent in making decisions concerning the firm in his final days. Roy listened but pretended to show more interest in viewing the memorabilia than what the man was suggesting. As he continued to speak, the glass doors swung open, and Mrs. Brimm came into the office to invite Roy to share some refreshments with the members. She took his arm and hurried him out of the office as he quickly looked over his shoulder and thanked Grazi for sharing his collection. The man grunted and slumped into the chair behind his desk, a frown framed his daring face.

When he was leaving, Mrs. Brimm rode with Roy in the elevator. She took the opportunity to ask him about his encounter with Jacob Grazi and was furious but not surprised when Roy gave an account of their somewhat brief meeting. He mentioned Grazi's accusation concerning her husband's sanity in his last days and the offer to buy him out. The good lady apologized for the manners of her cousin-in-law and business partner. She told Roy that Grazi held the smallest amount of shares in the firm and that her husband did not intend for him to ever have full control of the business. She went on to say that his past dealings with certain individuals connected to organized crime had ostensibly compromised the firm, almost costing it its reputation. But because he was the grandson of the founder of the business, nothing was done about it except the fact that he was never to inherit the firm.

As he drove out of the parking lot, Roy turned up the radio to clear his head a bit. For a moment, he thought that his mother's fears may have been justified. Nevertheless, he was committed to the idea of using most of his fortune to get that much needed extension of the hospital. That being his objective, he could ignore everything else and focus on his own work and family. Any thoughts he entertained involving the Brimm firm of architects and engineers in the project were quickly dismissed from his mind. His purpose was to donate the money and let the hospital go about their business of erecting the wing.

Jacob Grazi was determined to find out more about Dr. McPherson. He was skeptical about his relationship to Steven Brimm and, more so, the fact that he had inherited control of the firm. He had high expectations for his own future there, and that did not include having the doctor as a senior partner. Grazi was an ambitious fellow who had enough of towing the line since his brush with the law several years before. As the only other surviving male relative of the founder of the firm, he felt certain that his shares would increase after his cousin Steven Brimm died. That, however, did not happen, and it was all because of the stranger Dr. Roy McPherson, and it peeved Grazi. The next day, he called Roy, reiterating his offer to purchase his shares. Roy listened to what the man offered, then told him he would let him know when he made a decision concerning the offer. The conversation was brief and to the point. Roy did not wish to seem impolite by refusing to take the call; moreover, he had no intentions of feeling obliged to return a call to this man whom he felt a sudden disdain for. He just hoped he could settle the matter at hand as quickly as possible and never have to think about it again.

Throughout his workweek, Roy had an uneasy feeling about the man Jacob Grazi. He did not have the opportunity of speaking with his parents about the outcome of the board meeting or what transpired between him and Steven Brimm's cousin. In any case, he thought it best to approach Mrs. Brimm first since Grazi's offer for his shares exceeded what she was prepared to pay. Before he got around to doing so, he received a report from Dr. Burrows outlining his concerns and recommendations for Cara. The girl needed surgery and several months of rehab, but he was confident that she would walk normally. This was encouraging news, just what Roy needed to convey to the girl and her mother. As he sat at his desk going over the report and thinking how it would make a big difference in the life of such a beautiful girl, he remembered her father. Mr. Brimm certainly seemed proud of the girls and would want the best for Cara. Roy couldn't help feeling that the strange fate that brought them together had intervened in his life once more. In as much as he would have liked to shake off the Brimm family and their concerns, there was always something pulling him back in that direction. *Maybe I need to settle things quickly and be done with every matter of theirs that I have been involved with*, he thought.

That evening after dinner, Roy called Mrs. Brimm to let her know he was willing to go over the medical report with her and recommended that she bring the girl to his office the following afternoon. The middle-aged lady thanked the doctor for following up on the case and confessed that her efforts to encourage her daughter to see Dr. Burrows again were futile.

"I'm sure she would not mind seeing you though," Mrs. Brimm told Roy and suggested that if it was not too inconvenient for him, he was welcome to visit them any evening instead.

Roy was not bothered by her suggestion. As a matter of fact, he also saw it as an opportunity to deal with the question of Jacob Grazi since he would have the time to devote to both matters.

As he stood on the porch and rang the doorbell, a weird feeling came over Roy. He had not told his parents about Steve Brimm's handicapped daughter or that he had arranged a medical consultation for her. He felt as though he was getting involved with this family against his will and wondered what his mother would say if she knew. However, his thoughts were quickly disturbed by a noisy teen who opened the door while screaming for her mother.

"You certainly have good lungs," Roy told Jane as he stepped inside, but she merely smiled and pointed to the headphones she was wearing.

"Please have a seat!" she shouted while running off. "Mom will be down soon."

But Mrs. Brimm was already standing in the hallway, shaking her head and looking at her daughter. She greeted Roy and led him to the same room where they met once before.

"I think we will have a bit of peace and quiet in here," she said. "I wanted to talk to you before Cara comes in." Mrs. Brimm continued, "You see, she is unwilling to have any type of surgery, and I can't seem to convince her of it."

"Leave it to me," Roy said. "I will have a talk with her, but first let me go over the report with you."

He opened his briefcase and pulled out a folder and was thumbing through the pages when Cara entered the room. Her walk was slow and looked painful as she dragged her foot. She waited until she got close to Roy before greeting him.

"Are you OK?" he asked.

She appeared a bit more awkward than the first time he had seen her, but the girl simply said that some days were better than others.

"I was just going over Dr. Burrow's report with your mother, would you like to listen?" Roy asked, trying his best to put the girl at ease. She slumped down on the sofa beside her mother. Roy looked at her for a moment, then said, "Can you promise me one thing?"

"What's that?" she asked.

"When this is all over, will you dance with me?" he said, pointing to the folder on his lap.

The girl shrugged and grinned with embarrassment.

"Then I take it as yes," Roy said. "Now let's continue."

Using all his medical skills, Roy was careful to explain the necessity for surgery and the reasons for not procrastinating any longer. He also pointed out that Cara's rehabilitation would be complete and a lot smoother if she were to have corrective surgery before she got any older. In stressing that time was of the essence, he captured the girl's attention. Her mother had very little to say except to encourage her daughter to ask pertinent questions that would help her make a decision. When they had exhausted the subject, Cara excused herself and left the room. Her mother felt somewhat satisfied and invited Roy to stay for dinner. Although he saw it as a chance to switch the conversation to Jacob Grazi, he declined the invitation, saying he preferred to take a rain check instead. Mrs. Brimm thanked him for taking the time to talk with Cara and promised to let him know as soon as Dr. Burrows gave her a date for the surgery. Roy told her he would be in touch with her before then as he needed to settle affairs concerning the shares.

"And that brings me to the question of Jacob Grazi," he said promptly, then paused as he shifted papers together while putting away the folder.

"Is anything the matter?" she asked.

"Well, he continues to make bids for the shares," Roy told her.

"I hope you are not going to do business with that man," Mrs. Brimm cautioned.

"You tell me," he replied. "The man has been after me, offering large sums of money to buy me out of the inheritance. What should I do?"

Roy wanted to let her know that he was getting a better offer, but more than that, he wanted to know if there was something he needed to worry about.

Mrs. Brimm sighed, then said to Roy, "I can't stop you from doing what you want with your shares, but I can tell you this much. If Jake acquires a large chunk of your shares, he would ultimately own the firm. And since it has been the dying wish of my husband and his father before him that the firm remains with the descendants of Steven Brimm, it would be very dishonorable to ignore that."

Mrs. Brimm went on to tell Roy that Jacob Grazi would do all he could to attain ownership of the firm, even if it meant scaring him into turning over his shares if he thought that his price tag did not matter. She said that Grazi was not convinced that Roy was undeniably the son of Steven Brimm, and she was certain he would go out of his way to prove otherwise.

"You can't let him scare you," she said. "If you wish, I would be happy to intervene on your behalf. Leave Jake to me."

Roy thought for a moment, then told Mrs. Brimm he would much prefer if she appointed a time with the attorneys to settle the transfer of the shares as soon as possible.

"Pardon me for asking," she said. "But if you need such a large sum of money, I'm sure the bank would give you a loan using your shares as collateral."

Roy smiled and told her he preferred not.

"Well then," she said, "I guess I will have to be the new owner of the firm."

He thanked her and left.

On his way home, Roy thought about what Mrs. Brimm had to say about Jacob Grazi and wondered what his parents would think about the whole situation. He needed to talk things over with his father, so he picked up the phone as soon as he got home and called him. Sandy promised they would make the trip down to Hillcrest the next day and overnight the weekend. Roy felt relieved; he knew he could always rely on his parents' support. However, he was worried about his mother's concerns and what effect it may have on her when she heard about Jacob Grazi's envy. The man was some years younger than Steve Brimm, and Roy wondered if his mother ever knew of him. Maybe they attended the same school, or she may have met him at Steve's graduation party. Wild thoughts filled Roy's head as he tried to make sense of the whole bizarre affair.

The next evening, Roy arrived home to find his father playing with his grandson while his mother sat with Trudy, timing her pains. She was in the beginning stages of labor but did not want to rush to the hospital too early and decided not to let Roy know until he got home. Fiona seemed anxious; she was on the verge of calling her son but stopped when she noticed the car lights in the driveway. Roy wasted no time in getting his wife to the hospital. This was another distraction for him; all thoughts of previous events over the past weeks left his mind as he was about to become a father again.

Early the next morning, Trudy gave birth to a bouncing baby boy, but the happy occasion also brought back to mind the man they knew as Steven Brimm for this child was born with a scar on his hip. Although rather tiny, Roy and his mother knew that it would get bigger with time. His esteemed colleague Dr. Harris, who was the baby's pediatrician, offered to arrange a skin graft for the baby, but Roy refused.

Sandy and Fiona stayed a bit longer in Hillcrest until Trudy's mother arrived to help out with her homecoming. Roy was glad to have some time to get together with his parents and acquaint them on all that happened since they last met. He was hoping his mother may have had some knowledge about Steven Brimm's cousin Jacob Grazi, but that was not the case. She was quite annoyed that the man questioned Roy's identity and warned her son to have nothing to do with him. They were both happy that their son chose integrity over money and commended him for selling his shares back to the Brimm estate rather than to Jacob Grazi. Fiona did not comment on the situation concerning Cara. She simply listened, but her warm smile told her son that she had approved of him helping the girl to get the surgery she needed.

Back at the farm, preparations had begun for the upcoming wedding of Rory, which was to take place in a few weeks. Fiona spent her days sprucing up the house and making accommodations for her large family. At every moment, she worried about the safety of her son and his family. If Grazi was such an unscrupulous fellow, who knew how far he would go to ensure that Roy and his children surrender whatever inheritance they had? She was glad that Roy was getting rid of the bulk of it, but there was still a small portion of shares left in trust for his children, and her instincts told her that Grazi would resent every bit of it.

Having received a draft from the bank for the entire sum of money Mrs. Brimm paid in exchange for his shares, Roy donated it to the hospital in the name of Steven Brimm for the sole purpose of erecting a new wing. Only his parents knew of his generous deed, but they were unaware that the extension would be known as the Brimm Auditorium. Dr. Roy McPherson felt quite pleased and satisfied, having settled the matter sooner than he had expected. It had been some time since he was able to sit back and relax with his family and not think about the burden of his inheritance.

Two nights before his wedding, Rory and his brothers enjoyed an evening out in town. They were all having such a good time that no one noticed the bald chubby fellow who sat across from their table at the bar. He was accompanied by a young lady—much too young to be his wife, one would think. As the evening wore on and he had more than his share of booze, he became obnoxious, but the boys paid no attention to what was happening at the bar. When he was asked to leave the premises, the man got up and walked over to where the boys sat. As he looked up, Roy was amazed to see Jacob Grazi standing before him—his necktie in his hand and a young lady clinging to him as he swayed back and forth. His voice was loud as he spoke.

"Hello, Dr. Mac! Who's your company?" the man blurted out.

Roy was embarrassed. Nevertheless, he greeted Grazi and told him he was with his brothers, hoping the man would leave. But instead, he bent over, placing one hand on the table, and said sarcastically, "Are these the sons of Steve Brimm as well?"

Roy was silent while his brothers continued to chat and ignore the man.

"Did you share your inheritance with them?" Grazi blurted out again.

"I think you had better leave now," Roy told him quite forcefully, but the man became obnoxious again and accused Roy of forging his identity.

As the words came out of his mouth, Roy rose to his feet, his face red with anger as he struggled to control his temper. He calmly seized Grazi by the arm and led him to the gents' room. His brothers and the young lady looked on in amazement. Once inside, Roy pulled up his shirt and turned his back to Grazi as he removed his trousers, just enough so the man could have a clear view of the scar on his hip.

"You may touch it if you like," Roy said. "It's real. I was born with it, and so is my son."

Grazi stared at the scar but said nothing. Roy looked around to find him shivering and rubbing his cheeks. After fixing his clothing, Roy returned to his brothers and calmly sat down at the table.

"Well, I guess he won't be bothering us anymore," he said as he refreshed his glass of wine.

"What was that all about?" Rory asked.

"Oh, just an incoherent drunk," was Roy's reply, and his brothers laughed.

The revelation must have shocked the man into soberness for he quickly and quietly left the restaurant, walking quite steadily followed by his date.

It was already way past midnight, and the boys were still celebrating. Raymond suggested that they continue at a nearby nightclub, but Roy insisted that they call it a night and get some rest.

"What's up, big brother, aren't you on vacation?" Ray teased, but Roy simply smiled and said, "I promised Mom to keep you sober." So they decided to take his advice. Rory stayed with Ray and Ralphie at their city digs while Roy continued home.

After several hours of sleep, the three boys headed out to the farm later that morning. Fiona was relieved to see her sons arrive safely and ordered them to wash up while she fixed lunch. Having slept much too late to have breakfast, the boys were famished and welcomed the hot lunch. They were in good spirits and joked with one another as they ate. Fiona was still in the kitchen getting lunch for Sandy when she overheard them joking about the man Roy pushed into the washroom.

"Maybe he was going to show him his inheritance." Ralphie laughed as he uttered the words, and his brothers kicked him under the table, signaling that their mother was around.

Fiona was a bit disturbed by what she overheard but refrained from questioning her sons as she did not want them to know that she was listening. Instead, she hurried them up and sent them out to help their dad so he could come in and have lunch. When they were gone, she called Roy to let him know what she had heard and to find out what he told them. Roy was amused. He told her about running into a drunken Jacob Grazi who casually asked if he had shared his inheritance with his brothers.

"What about you pushing him into the washroom?" his mother asked.

"Oh, that was just to calm him down. Now, Mom, just don't get any more ideas. I'm sure the boys would soon forget all about it," Roy said.

Fiona was not convinced but decided to take her son's advice and not dwell on the subject any longer. Roy had promised to come by the day before the wedding to help his brother Raymond with transportation for their grandmother and Aunt Violet's trip out to the farm. He was hoping to have some more time alone with his brothers since he knew it would worry his mother if they were to make fun of him in her presence. *Though quite innocent of the circumstances, it would nevertheless lead to some embarrassment,* he thought.

Roy, Ray, and the old ladies arrived at the farm at noon the next day. It was a hot, muggy afternoon, and the old girls were simply exhausted from the trip. The boys helped with getting them settled comfortably inside while their mother poured ice tea for everyone. After lunch, the boys went to collect their tuxedos for the wedding. On the way back, they stopped at a local pub to have a pint and play a bit of pool. Roy was a bit hesitant at first but decided to go along with his brothers who were delighted to have him with them.

"This feels like old times!" Rory exclaimed. "I don't know when we last got together like this to play a game."

The four sat in a booth facing one another, sipping cold beer and reminiscing about their college days when Raymond told Roy about Ralphie's silly comment the day before. Roy blushed, then said to his youngest brother, "You better not make such comments around Mom. As a matter of fact, I want you all to forget you ever saw that man and never joke about it again."

Roy was serious as he spoke, and his brothers looked at one another for answers.

"Why, who is that man?" Rory asked.

"Well, it's a long story, and I have no desire to go into it now," Roy told them and then Ralphie asked what it had to do with inheritance.

Roy sighed. He looked at his brothers, their questioning faces gazing at him in innocent adoration, melting his heart and filling him with emotion.

He bent his head and let his forehead rest softly on his uplifted fingertips, his thoughts intense for a moment. Then breaking the silence, he said softly, "I have something to tell you, guys, but first you have to give me your word not to let Mom or Dad know what I'm about to tell you. It really isn't a big secret. I know Mom will let you know in her own time, but until then, just keep it to yourselves for now."

The boys listened as Roy told them that their dad was not his biological father. He told them that he was adopted as a baby by Sandy when their parents married and confessed that he was just as surprised as they were to discover that fact. Rory was exceedingly curious when he heard that Roy had the opportunity of being acquainted with his biological father before he died. He wanted to know what his brother knew about the man and was amazed when Roy admitted that he knew very little until he was left an inheritance. Roy was careful not to disclose details surrounding his birth, but he did reveal that apart from their dad, no one in the family knew who his biological father was and that their mother wanted to keep it that way.

It was a lot for the boys to process; they seemed a bit perplexed and asked about the man they encountered in the restaurant. Ralphie was curious about his reference to an inheritance and questioned his brother.

"I'll get to that," Roy said. He finished his beer, pushed the bottle aside, and gave a tight-lipped grin. After a brief silence, he said, "Jacob Grazi is the black sheep cousin of my biological father and is unhappy that I have inherited the wealth he obviously thought was his. He is not convinced that I am the true son of his cousin. He was trying to buy all the shares in the company I have inherited so he could own it outright. The man is a very persistent fellow. I have the feeling that he would stop at nothing to get what he's after, and I'm a bit bothered by him. That is why I have decided to dump all the inheritance, except for a small portion that is put aside for my boys—"

Roy could not finish speaking because Ralphie interrupted impatiently. "You mean to say you are very rich?"

"No," Roy replied. "You can say I was a very wealthy man for a short while, but now I'm just a regular hardworking guy like before."

"What do you mean when you said you dumped it?" Ralphie asked again.

"Well, I sold my interest in the company and donated the money to charity," Roy explained.

"All of it?" asked Ralphie.

"Yes," Roy said.

"But why?" continued Ralphie. "Why would you do a dumb thing like that?"

"Oh shut up, Ralph," Rory chimed in. "You ask too many questions. Did Mom and Dad know about it?"

"Yes," Roy replied. "Mom was just as skeptical as I was about accepting such a large inheritance from a man I hardly knew, but Dad thought it was my birthright and influenced me to accept it if only to pass it on to my children. But I could never have kept it. That man Jacob Grazi was after me, he made handsome offers."

"Did you sell to him?" Rory asked.

"No, I sold to the rightful heirs."

Roy did not want to elaborate, but his brothers asked in unison, "Who's that?"

"The surviving spouse, a very wealthy woman," Roy said slowly. Then he got up and told his brothers that they had spent enough time at the pub.

Roy sat in front next to Rory, who was driving, while Raymond and Ralphie sat in the back of the truck. An uncomfortable silence prevailed as the four brothers sped down the road. Roy did not know what to make of it; he loved his brothers but wondered if they were seeing him in a different light. *Only time will tell*, he thought. As if to read his mind, the questions came tumbling out again. This time, it was Raymond who wanted to know if his brother kept any money for himself. Roy told him he kept not a penny.

"Why didn't you keep some for us?" he joked. But Roy made it quite clear that neither he nor their parents would be at ease with such a decision.

Then Ralphie added, "Hey, big brother, I need a Porsche. You could have bought me one."

"Why would he get you a Porsche to drive around *Fusty Sally* in?" Raymond said, tapping his brother on his head.

"Who is that?" Roy asked, looking around and smirking at his brothers.

"His new gal," Raymond said, and the three laughed.

"I must meet her. Is she coming to the wedding?" Roy asked.

"What wedding? Not mine!" Rory snuffled, and the boys burst into laughter again.

After a lot of jovial chatter, the truck turned into the driveway, and the boys were reminded about the promise they made to their eldest brother. While Rory and Raymond hurried into the house with the clothing bags,

Roy took his time walking with his arm around Ralphie as he cautioned him about making silly fun of the situation concerning their encounter with Grazi and the newfound knowledge about his inheritance and birth.

"I know Mom and Dad would talk about it in their own time, but for now, just keep a lid on your enthusiasm. Would you do that for me?" Roy asked his brother.

"Yes, oh yes, you don't have to worry, but it will cost you." Ralphie smiled broadly at his brother as he spoke.

"Well, are you going to bring what's-her-name Sally to the wedding?" Roy asked.

The two walked to the back of the house and stood at the bottom of the stairs.

"I don't know about that," said Ralphie.

"Why is that?" Roy asked.

His brother's face got quite serious as he explained that the girl he had been dating for several months was not known to any of the family and was very humble.

"Don't get me wrong!" he was quick to clarify. "She is very beautiful and smart, but she is a bit old-fashioned. She was orphaned at ten and grew up with two old aunts who took good care of her and made sure she graduated college. Now she helps take care of them, and that seems to be the problem."

"Why is that?" Roy's curiosity seemed to build as he asked the question, but Ralphie took some time to answer as he hammered his heel into the dirt.

"It's a bit embarrassing," he said after a while. "Once I complimented her on a dress she was wearing, she said it previously belonged to her aunt. They seem to have a great influence on how she dresses and does her hair, even her cologne smells like theirs. I just don't get it, and I can't have her come to the wedding like that."

Roy smiled as he listened to his youngest brother. Then he suggested that he consider taking his date shopping for the occasion and maybe presenting her with some fresh cologne.

"If you do consider it, let me know," Roy said. "I know just the place you could take her to find beautiful clothing in such short time."

"But what about Rory?" Ralphie asked, shaking his head from side to side.

"Just leave him to me," Roy said. "If you really would like her to come to the wedding, I will sort that out with Mom and Dad, but you don't have much time to make that decision. Let me know before I go home, and I would make arrangements with my sister-in-law to have her boutique outfit Sally in the morning."

Ralphie thanked his brother and pushed open the door, and they entered the kitchen where their mother, grandmother, and Aunt Violet sat at a table folding laundry.

Chapter 13
The Gift Box

It was Tuesday morning. The sky was bright and sunny; the farmhouse was calm once again after a festive weekend of friends and family who gathered for Rory's wedding. Fiona stood at the window looking on as workmen dismantled a tent, which was erected for an outdoor picnic the day after the wedding. She felt satisfied and relieved that the hustle and bustle was over, and everyone pretty much enjoyed themselves. Sandy and Ralphie left earlier that morning to take her mother and aunt back to Hillcrest. With Rory and his wife off on their honeymoon and Raymond filling in for him at the factory, Fiona was left to keep an eye on the workers, making sure that everything was put back in order.

Back in Hillcrest, Roy prepared himself for a hectic workweek after a short vacation. He was optimistic and bubbly at the beginning of the week, but a call from Mrs. Brimm interrupted his bright mood when she asked if she could visit him anytime soon.

"I have a gift for the baby and would like to deliver it to you before we go to New York."

"Is Cara having her operation?" Roy asked.

"Yes, she will be admitted to a hospital next week," the lady said nervously.

"Oh I see," he said. "Well, maybe I could drop by to see her before you leave."

"That would be nice," Mrs. Brimm replied. "I'm sure she would like that."

Roy thanked her for calling and told her that he would call before dropping in.

In the meantime, meetings had begun to take place for electing a suitable committee to oversee the planning and erecting of the new hospital wing. As a contributor, Dr. McPherson was the first one elected to the committee. He felt honored and knew that it would mean a lot of extra work, so he graciously declined the offer but promised to have an input should they need his advice anytime.

Everything seems to be falling slowly into place, Roy thought. He had not heard from Jacob Grazi anymore, and that in itself was a relief. The Friday that followed, he called Mrs. Brimm to let her know that he was stopping by to see Cara. He had purchased a book on dancing from the local bookstore for her to pass the time in the hospital. He remembered the promise he made to her and hoped that it would give her courage. At that time, Roy allowed his wife and children to accompany him on the visit. He knew that Mrs. Brimm truly wanted to see his sons, and he did not wish to deny her that opportunity since she was a very honest and forthright lady with a courteous personality.

When they arrived at the house, they were greeted at the door by Cara. Her large brown eyes lit up at the sight of the children.

"Can I hold the baby?" she asked, looking pleadingly at Trudy.

Both Trudy and Roy smiled and quickly glanced at each other.

"Hold on, hold on," Cara said softly. "I have to sit first."

She invited them into the family room, hobbling along in front of them with an uneasy gait. "You can sit wherever you like," she said to Roy and Trudy as she slumped into a soft burgundy recliner and prepared to take the baby.

Just then, her mother entered the room; a look of surprise defined her face. Trudy straightened up after placing the baby in Cara's arms, and Roy made the introductions.

"How kind of you to come," she told Trudy. "I am pleased to meet your family," the good lady told Roy.

Having invited them to sit and be comfortable, she excused herself to get refreshments. While she was gone, Roy tried to engage Cara in a conversation about her trip to New York, but she did not respond. He told her that her decision was a good one and that she would be in very good hands, but the young lady was not interested is speaking about the operation. She seemed nervous and distracted by the baby in her arms.

Sensing her anxiety about the subject, Trudy quickly interrupted, "You may come and visit the baby when you get back from New York." Cara's eyes lit up once more.

"Really?" she said as she looked questioningly at Trudy. "I will have to do a lot of therapy, but I would love to see him when it's all over."

"OK then, we have a date," Trudy replied.

The loud sound of the doorbell startled the baby. Trudy quickly took him from Cara who then begged little Rickey to sit with her, but the child was shy and hung on to his father.

"Will you get that, Mom?" Cara said to her mother who was just entering the room with a tray of cookies. Placing the tray on a side table next to little Rickey, she went to open the door.

Jane entered the house followed by a few noisy teenagers; their laughter and chattering brought Roy back to his own teenage days, growing up with his brothers. The young girl did not seem interested in the visitors; she merely shouted hello and waved her hand before disappearing into the house followed by her two friends.

"Don't worry, one day she will be a lady," her mother said as she began serving refreshments.

After returning home from their short visit with the Brimm family, Roy sat in his study, his eyes fixed on the documents in the rectangular gift box that Trudy had just unwrapped. A dull feeling swept over him that left him in somewhat of a daze.

"What's wrong?" Trudy asked. "Those are bonds, are they not? And from the inscriptions, they are for both our sons, are they not?"

Roy sighed, pinched his chin, then looked at his wife for a long moment before saying, "He wrote this, this is his handwriting. I recognize it from a letter he wrote."

"What letter?" Trudy asked. "What are you talking about, Roy? Whose handwriting is it?"

Roy sat silently for a while. Then removing the documents from the box, he said softly, "These bonds were purchased by Steven Brimm himself. He probably did so after meeting his grandson for the first and only time. It is intended for Rickey and his siblings. But why such an enormous amount? He knew what he was doing with his will, why did he feel it necessary to endow our children like this? He must have presumed that I would renounce his inheritance. I'm sure he wanted his wife to hang on to this gift until the children got older, but I am assuming that because of the trust fund that was set up for them, she felt she could depart with it sooner."

Trudy watched as her husband tucked the documents back into the gift box, then asked, "What are we to do now?"

"Ah! Just leave it. I'll put it away for them," the young doctor said.

The couple enjoyed a quiet dinner after putting their children to bed. There wasn't too much conversation between them as they both wondered about their children's future. Roy, more than Trudy, was very uncomfortable with this sudden wealth that the children obviously would inherit as young adults and was determined to keep that knowledge from them until he felt they were mature enough to make competent decisions. He expressed his concern to Trudy and made her promise to do the same. The question now was, Should he share this new knowledge with his parents? That was something Roy refused to be indecisive about.

The following week, Cara, accompanied by her mother and sister, was admitted to a hospital in New York. Dr. Burrows spoke with Dr. McPherson after several hours of surgery and assured him that the patient was doing well and the surgery successful. He also explained that she would have to remain in the hospital a bit longer and had advised her mother that her first few weeks of therapy should be done at a facility in New York. Thereafter, she may continue therapy in her hometown. He informed Roy that he would be releasing Cara into the care of Dr. Harmon at Hillcrest Hospital when the time came for her to return home. Roy was pleased and relieved at the news; he was especially grateful that Dr. Harmon would be following the girl's progress. Roy sensed that he was growing fond of those girls but could not explain such a feeling. *Was it because they were left to grow up without a father?* he thought. After all, they were not even half sisters of his, not by a long shot. However, he quickly pushed those thoughts aside to focus on important matters. With the Brimm family out of town and Jacob Grazi out of his hair, there would be no sudden surprises on the horizon, or so he thought.

The day was hardly over when Roy received a phone call from his mother. Rory was back from his honeymoon, and Raymond had returned to Hillcrest. With very little to occupy her, Fiona's mind traveled far and wide; now her focus was once again on Roy. Although he welcomed her calls, he had become a bit tired of reassuring his mother that he was in no present danger. Nevertheless, she had a sixth sense, and she was right. There was reason to be cautious about the man Jacob Grazi, and Roy was soon to find out more about this sinister fellow.

The Brimm home remained vacant while the family spent time in New York, and Grazi saw it as an opportunity to gather information. So he broke into the residence in search of any clue or other valuable material he could find to use in his quest to bring down Dr. McPherson. After carefully combing the attic, a place he thought his cousin would store old memoirs, he turned his attention to the desk drawers in the study room. He was careful not to leave anything out of place. He wore gloves and only focused his attention on places he thought would have important papers or documents. However, his efforts were futile, and frustration overcame him, but he was determined to find something that linked the young doctor to the family. If he could only prove that Dr. McPherson is truly an heir of Steven Brimm, then he would go ahead with his sordid plan of blackmailing him out of all the money he received for the shares he sold before finishing him off. Yes, Grazi had a plan for Roy, and he was not going to let anyone interfere with it. No, not like Roy interfered with his plan for the company.

While speaking all these thoughts to himself, he reached for a shelf in which Steven Brimm kept photo albums. These were still in their old place as he remembered them when he visited his cousin in their younger years. After going through several pages of photos, he reached up to put back the albums, and a small brown official envelope shifted on the shelf. He grabbed the envelope and removed a folded photocopy of a birth certificate from it. Grazi stared at the paper intently. "But who was Fiona Leighton?" he muttered to himself. Then observing the date of birth of a baby boy, he had a sudden rush of enthusiasm. "Maybe this is it," he grunted loudly, then impulsively looked around to see if anyone heard him. The man knew that the possibility of anyone returning home to find him in the house was very remote; nevertheless, he had a plan in place just in case.

Jacob Grazi put back the empty envelope on the shelf and tucked the folded paper into his pocket. He snatched a torchlight and headed for the attic again, his thoughts racing as he went through boxes in search of the one that contained old high school yearbooks of the Brimms. He took another glance at the paper to make sure he remembered the name of the person he was looking for. Then diving into the box, he came out with a high school yearbook of the graduating class of 1958. He carefully scrutinized the pages until he found Fiona's name and photograph. Grazi felt quite satisfied with himself. He sprawled on the floor thinking that his cousin was once mixed up with this girl, and the result had to be Dr. McPherson. But he could not understand why Steven Brimm's name was not recorded on the paper he had in his pocket. It was something he vowed to find out, but how?

It was getting late, and the man became conscious of the length of time he had spent in the house. He was a bit concerned that his car might be noticed even though he parked it down the block, so he dusted himself off and carefully left through the front door after securing the patio door he entered through. He was satisfied to some extent with his mission but still needed valuable information to fill in the missing pieces of the puzzle.

Over the course of the next few days, Grazi hired a private investigator; he wanted to find out all he could about Roy. He was certain that Mrs. Brimm knew the whole story and despised her for not letting the board of directors know about Roy sooner. However, apart from matters pertaining to company business, she seldom ever spoke to the man and had very little contact with him since her husband died. She was a simple but powerful woman, and Grazi knew that he needed to toe the line if there was any likelihood of him taking command of the company in the future.

It didn't take long for him to receive enough information to set his plan of extortion into motion. He had one of his thugs call Roy, accusing him of being the bastard son of Steven Brimm who came out of the woodwork to deprive the rightful heirs of their fortune. The man on the phone said he needed fifty thousand dollars for this information and was prepared to sell it if Roy did not come up with the cash soon enough. Roy had no chance to respond. The caller simply hung up the phone after saying he would contact him again in a few days. *This is absurd*, Roy thought. *Who would do a thing like this?* However, he did not have to search for the answer; he knew that only one person could be behind such a call.

It was already late afternoon. Roy was angry, but he focused on his patients and tried to forget about the call. On his way home, he remembered his mother's concerns and knew he had to do something about Jacob Grazi. He had no intentions of enlightening his wife or parents on this situation. He had to find a way to deal with it, so he waited for a few days to see if the caller would try to contact him again. It was not easy to get in touch with Roy by phone at the hospital. Furthermore, when he was in his office, only his immediate family would be put through. Therefore, the caller had to have known when to call and who to impersonate to be able to speak directly with the doctor. Consequently, Roy gave strict instructions to his office staff that if any member of his family wanted to speak to him, they must leave a number, and he would call them right back. He also secretly recorded phone calls at his office and residence.

One windy afternoon, two days after the call, the doctor sat at his desk thumbing through a few notes that were placed there by his secretary. One listed a call from his brother, but the number was unfamiliar, so he put that note in his pocket and continued with appointments for the day. Later that evening, while Trudy spent some time putting the children to bed, Roy called Jacob Grazi. The man pretended to be surprised to hear from Roy and asked what he could do for him.

"You could listen to what I have to say and put an end to those harassing phone calls. I don't take kindly to blackmail, Mr. Grazi," Roy said.

"I have no idea what you're talking about, Dr. Mac, could you enlighten me?" said Grazi.

"Oh, I think you do," Roy continued. "I also know the feds would welcome another chance to investigate certain individuals in the Brimm company if only for blackmail."

"Are you threatening me?" Grazi clenched his teeth as he spoke.

"Call it what you like," Roy replied. "But if I receive any more calls or notes with a hint of blackmail, or if anyone harasses my family, the feds will know about it. That's all I wanted to say, Mr. Grazi, have a good evening." Roy paused, then hung up the phone.

He could hear the heavy breathing of an astounded individual before he ended the call. Grazi was a bit apprehensive since he had no idea how much Roy knew about his previous brush with the feds or if he knew anything at all. It was now time for the doctor to wait and see what the next move will be. He looked at the note he had in his pocket, then locked it in his desk drawer before retiring for the night. His instinct told him not to destroy that note; the phone number on it may come in handy.

The rest of that week went without incident. The good doctor threw himself into his work with more determination and zeal. He was good at his vocation and was renowned not only for his skill as a doctor but also for his quiet compassion, yet it seemed his rewards in life were more than he bargained for. Virgil once said, "Whatever it be, every fortune is to be overcome by bearing it," and his was no exception. Much was at stake, and Roy was not prepared to be intimidated in any way. He had given much consideration to the reality that it could well be dangerous to have an enemy like Jacob Grazi. After all, "a man cannot be too careful in the choice of his enemies," to quote Oscar Wilde.

Meanwhile, Grazi had started to rethink his plan. He made his thug hold off on any more calls to the doctor, deciding that something more forceful needed to be done if he was to succeed in recovering any part of what he deemed to be his fortune. He was not afraid to go after the doctor and did not once stop to consider that he was also a relative. That thought never entered the man's head; he was already peeved that he had to share with two children who did not even have Brimm's bloodline.

It has been three weeks since Cara's operation, and reports said she was progressing very well with her therapy. Mrs. Brimm called Roy to let him know that her daughter was soon scheduled to be transferred to Hillcrest Hospital, and she will be returning in a few days to make arrangements. Roy welcomed the opportunity to have a chat with the lady. He thought she needed to know about the phone calls and his conversation with Jacob Grazi, which incidentally he had recorded.

"If you let me know when you will be in town, I will drop around to see you," he told her.

"I will call again as soon as we arrive. It will be nice seeing you," the elderly lady replied.

"Good, I'll be expecting it," Roy said and thanked her.

That weekend, he visited the farm with his family. He had not been there since Rory's wedding. He also surprised his parents by taking his grandmother and Aunt Violet for the ride. It was good for the doctor to get away for a while since it seemed as though the town of Hillcrest was closing in on him. Funny how one sinister fellow like Jacob Grazi could have such an effect on the lives of so many! Roy did not want to talk about the man or even think about him that weekend; he just wanted to enjoy time with his parents and made sure he took his grandmother and aunt along so no one would dare discuss the Brimms or Grazi in their presence.

It turned out to be a relaxing and enjoyable time for the whole family. Fiona took care of her grandchildren while Roy, Rory, and their father played pool. The old ladies stuffed themselves with so much fresh berries that they both got sick. It was impossible for Aunt Violet to get out of her chair without sounding like an old car with engine trouble. As for Grandma Elsie, she collapsed on the couch without even knowing that she was sitting on the new hat she wore to church that morning. Fiona was a bit concerned about them, but having her son—a doctor—close at hand was some reassurance.

As they traveled back home on a warm Sunday evening, Roy noticed that a sudden warning light flashed on his dashboard just minutes away from the farm. He pulled into the nearest gas station to check on it and was relieved to find out that nothing was wrong with his engine, but the light kept flashing each time he stepped on the brake. So deciding not to take the chance of driving it for another two hours and also heeding the advice of an old mechanic from a nearby farm who had been there attending to his truck, he decided to call his father. Sandy was quick to arrive along with Rory. Not wanting to alarm the old ladies, Rory and Roy exchanged vehicles, and Sandy hooked up Roy's shiny sedan to his pickup and took it back to the farm. Before they continued on their journey, Rory promised his brother to take the car to the closest dealership and have them check it out the next morning.

"I'll call you when it's all done!" shouted Rory to his brother who had begun pulling out of the gas station.

Apart from the steady flow of soft music from the radio, the trip continued in total silence. Grandma Elsie and Aunt Violet slept all the way while Trudy nodded occasionally. However, Roy could not help thinking about his car and was somewhat upset that he did not have the time to look at it himself since he was certain he could find the fault. But then he thought that taking it to the dealership would be the best thing since he had recently purchased a more spacious vehicle to accommodate his growing family.

Early the next morning, Rory towed the car to a dealership in a nearby town. He was not lucky to get an immediate appointment, so he left the car and returned to the farm. He contacted Roy and gave him all the details for him to check on it as well. The doctor was busy as usual with his rounds for the morning, but the first chance he got, he called about his car, only to be told that he needed to be present at the repair shop as soon as possible. After explaining his situation, Roy demanded some information. The man at the other end of the line sounded matter-of-fact. "I can tell you what's wrong, sir, but this is a matter for the insurance company, as well as the police. So you should come and see for yourself before we go ahead with any repairs." Roy was puzzled. He thanked the man and told him he would send his brother over immediately.

Both Rory and Sandy arrived within the hour at the repair shop. They were given an account of the inspection and were told that the car was maliciously tampered with. And since it was under warranty, it would be appropriate to make a formal complaint about the malicious intent. It was only a matter of a few more miles before the brake line snapped fully, paving the way for a terrible accident.

After the initial shock, Rory glanced back at his father and asked, "Who would do this, Dad?"

Sandy's stare was vacant, but he knew full well who. He had heard his wife's concerns many a night about the envy over their son's inheritance, but he never thought it would come to this.

He stood in silence, just shaking his head as he looked intently at the exposed engine of the car. Then turning to the mechanic, he said, "I will have to notify my son, and we'll take it from there. I suggest we just leave things as they are for now until he contacts you."

"That's fine, but don't leave it too long. Our shop's crowded as it is," the man said with a sigh.

Sandy was not much for conversation on their way back to the farm; he wondered how his son would take this news. Such an incident was a direct attempt on his life and the lives of his family as well. He certainly did not deserve to be beleaguered in any way. Sandy was genuinely worried for Roy. He was also afraid to let Fiona know about this new development. She worried enough about the situation already, and he knew he had to find a way to keep it from her. While all these thoughts were racing around in his head, Rory was constantly trying to get his father's attention. He kept asking questions referring to Roy's inheritance; none of which Sandy heard. Eventually, he came to the conclusion that his father was not aware of Roy's inheritance and decided to shut up. As they drove up the driveway, Sandy cautioned Rory not to give his mother any information about the car other than it was still under repair and also indicated that he would speak to Roy himself about the situation.

Sandy never entered the house; he walked over to the factory where he locked himself in the office and called Roy. It took awhile before the doctor responded to his father's call, but when he did and was told about the outcome of the inspection, he was audibly angry.

"I take it this has something to do with that man Grazi?" his father asked quietly.

"I intend to prove it does," Roy replied. "And I will contact the repair shop and request a detailed report of their findings so I can proceed with a criminal investigation."

"Let me know what you need me to do," Sandy said. "I guess your brother will be asking many questions, just be prepared."

"I expect so," Roy said. "I will discuss it with Rory, Dad. You can tell him I'll need his help."

"Well, that's fine, son, but no need to get Mother all upset. So whatever you two discuss, make sure he keeps it to himself. This is becoming a serious situation that has to be forcefully dealt with."

Sandy composed himself before returning to the house. The thought of what lay ahead for his son deeply disturbed him. Lunch was ready, so he washed up, sat next to Rory at the kitchen table, and read the newspaper while Fiona placed a few dishes in front of them.

"Did you have Roy's car fixed?" Fiona asked casually as she spooned some beans onto a plate.

"It's being done," Sandy answered quickly. "They may have to replace a few parts, so it will take some time." Looking up at Rory, he said, "You must call your brother this evening and let him know it will be all right for him to keep your car. He will be expecting it, you can use mine." Rory nodded and grunted; his mouth was full—very convenient—and his father smiled.

Roy had just arrived home that evening when the phone rang.

"Rory's on the phone!" Trudy shouted. "Should I tell him to call later?"

"No, no, I'll take it, hang on," Roy responded, hurrying into the house.

He wasted no time in discussing his plans for Grazi with his brother and asked him to pick up the report from the repair shop the next day and bring it with him. Roy had already appointed a private investigator and planned on paying a visit to the Hillcrest Police Station armed with the report and all the information he could gather concerning the threats to him and his family.

Mrs. Brimm and Jane arrived in Hillcrest that Monday evening. Roy was relieved when she contacted him early the following morning. He wanted to speak with her privately before calling in the authorities, so he went to see her as soon as Rory arrived with the report of the car. The elderly lady listened with openness as the young doctor revealed every encounter he had with Jacob Grazi and the thugs he hired to extort him. He showed her the report explaining that his car had been tampered with and told her he was adamant in his quest to prove that the man was involved.

"If you can help in any way with this investigation, I will be most grateful," Roy said. "I know you are quite familiar with his character, and I hope you will be willing to make a statement if needed."

Mrs. Brimm nodded. She was not very surprised that Jacob Grazi would go to such lengths but hoped that he possessed the sagacity to know better than to challenge a blood relative. "Of course I will help in any way I can," she said. "But for the sake of the company, I will have to be very discreet."

"I understand that," Roy said. "Since this is a sticky affair, it would be prudent not to let Mr. Grazi know that you are aware of the situation. I don't want your safety to be compromised in any way. Just let me deal with him myself, and while I am doing so, forgive me if I choose not to return to this house." "We will meet at the hospital, if that is all right?"

Mrs. Brimm confirmed, "Yes, of course, I look forward to seeing you there. Now tell me about Cara."

Roy pulled a pen from his pocket and began to scribble on a piece of paper as he spoke. "Take this," he said, handing the paper to Mrs. Brimm. "You can go to the nurses' station there to have me paged whenever you are in the hospital."

Rory played with his nephews while waiting for his brother at the house. When Roy arrived, the two left to call on the police chief at the Hillcrest Police Station. Roy was acquainted with the man who was a member of his golf club and whom he occasionally had a game with, so it was not very difficult to get an appointment that day. Chief Wells was a burly middle-aged man with a thin mustache and a husky voice. He welcomed Roy and Rory and invited them to sit in his office while he poured coffee. Roy did not wish to seem impolite, but he preferred to skip the chitchat and get right down to business.

"What can I do for you, Doctor?" the chief said finally.

"Well, I would like to make a formal complaint about a very serious matter concerning extortion and an attempt on my life."

The chief's eyebrows rose, and his eyes opened wide in surprise. He listened attentively as the doctor recounted the harassment by Grazi and the potential threats to him and his family.

After reading the report from the auto repair shop, Chief Wells told Roy he would like him to fill out some paperwork so that he can file a complaint.

"Don't worry too much," he said. "I will have my team on this right away. If my memory serves me correctly, I think the name Jacob Grazi came up in a federal investigation some years back. I will most certainly check on it, just leave it to me. You must arrange to bring your car into town as soon as possible so it can be inspected."

The chief opened a drawer and took out a blue and white business card and handed it to Roy. "I will tell them to expect it," he said. "And don't worry, it will be safe here."

Roy glanced at the card that contained the name and address of an auto repair shop in Hillcrest. He did not mention the private investigator he hired; he thought it best to keep that private.

"I can have the car here in the morning." Rory looked at his brother for acknowledgment as he spoke.

"That's good. I will have them alert me when it arrives."

"Thanks very much for all your help." Roy rose to his feet with an outstretched hand. "I must get back to the hospital."

Chief Wells shook Roy's hand with both of his; his grip was firm, his hands heavy. He gave a reassuring smile to the doctor as he said good day again.

It was early afternoon. Roy hurried back to the hospital to take over from Dr. Harmon, who graciously relieved him. Just knowing that he was finally going to get on with his life without having to bother about the inheritance or Jacob Grazi was a cheerful thought, but Roy was not naive. If anything substantial arose from this investigation, it would entail the court's involvement, and having that to deal with was sobering in itself.

Roy arrived home later than usual that evening, feeling quite satisfied about his day. It was a long day that ended with the groundbreaking ceremony for the new hospital wing. Pulling into the driveway, he noticed a shadow crouched at the side of his garage. He flashed his bright lights, and the bent-over figure of a man straightened up. He had a small flashlight in his hand. Roy remained in the car but rolled down the window as the man approached him.

"Mr. Lucky, what are you doing here?"

Recognizing the man to be the private investigator he hired, Roy turned off the engine and got out of the car.

"I wanted to check your garage without being noticed. There may be a possibility that your car was tampered with here, and if so, I will find clues," Lucky said.

"My garage is always locked, but you are welcome to have a look around." Roy pressed the remote and opened the door. He allowed the stocky, well-dressed man to enter and scrutinize it before he parked the car. However, there was no evidence that anyone forcibly tried to enter the garage.

"Tomorrow, I will check the staff parking at the hospital," Lucky said as he closed the gate behind him. "Will let you know what I come up with, doc."

Roy nodded, then watched the man disappear into the night before entering the house.

The next day, Mr. Lucky used his influence to gain access to the private parking facility for the medical personnel at the hospital. He scoured the area, making notes of security cameras and their locations. Through his good connections, he was able to take a look at some of the tapes that recorded cars going in and out of the garage a few days before the doctor's car troubles began. All the vehicles coming and going and their parking locations remained the same for all the days, with the exception of one day that recorded a burgundy early-model Mercedes with a license plate beginning with the acronym MD entering and leaving the garage.

Upon further investigation, Lucky observed that the car entered the garage at three o'clock in the afternoon on Friday, two days before Roy traveled out to the farm. He felt that he was on to something when he checked the log and noticed that the car had only made an entrance for a very brief time, hardly enough time for anyone using the skywalk to enter the hospital and return to where the car was parked. Lucky got very suspicious and did his best to obtain a copy of that particular tape, which he took to his lab for analysis. But try as he did, he was unable to identify the driver of the vehicle since the windows were tinted. However, an enlargement of the object revealed that the rear license plate—which shifted a bit, probably from driving—concealed another plate. The number of which was not visible.

There was little to go on. The spot that was exposed on the plate beneath had what looked like the very top of a figure four, which brought Lucky to the conclusion that the number below had to end with four. Taking a closer look at the car as it exited the garage, he noticed that it could have been driven by someone who was not too familiar with the exit ramp since it came very close to the unusual turn, grazing the steel pole as it sped away. The investigator felt this warranted more research. He was not contented with the analysis of the tape alone, so he paid another visit to the garage.

This time, he decided to test out the time it took to get from the parking lot to the hospital and back. While doing so, he noticed another security camera; this one was focused on the entrance of the skywalk, but Lucky did not recall seeing that tape. The automatic doors opened as he approached the entrance of the hospital. Stepping inside, he made a few steps forward, then turned, and exited again. The time—taken upon entering the garage, parking, and walking to the hospital and back to his car—was eight and a half minutes with brisk walking. Yet the log recorded the Mercedes leaving at three minutes after three. What happened there? Lucky was sure he would find some answer in the missing tape. So with some conviction, he was able to motivate the security office into a thorough search for the missing data. It seemed like a gargantuan effort, but the result was worth the worry. Tucked away at the back of a small cabinet was a piece of vital evidence that gave a visible account of people using the skywalk on the day in question. Again, the investigator was able to obtain a copy of the tape, which he hurriedly took to his lab.

The walkway was always busy, but there were times when few people used it, especially during midmorning and after lunch—as Lucky gathered from the tape. He narrowed his search by focusing on personnel going to the hospital and returning to the garage during the hour the Mercedes entered. Doctors, nurses, hospital staff, a few white coats, several suited men—all appearing to be quite normal. Just as he was about to call it a day, something caught his eye. It was the figure of a man in white overalls carrying what looked like a small wooden toolbox in his hand. He crossed the walkway at exactly three fifteen that afternoon and entered the hospital. Since that tape covered a twenty-four-hour period, Lucky decided to check further to see when the individual returned to the garage, but he did not. It seemed strange to the investigator. If he was parked there, why did he not return to his car? Maybe he wasn't parked in the garage since the individual was obviously not hospital personnel. Lucky sifted through all this information, formulating every scenario, then finally came up with the possibility that another exit may have been used.

It's back to the drawing board, another trip to the security office, he thought. But first, he wanted to get a bit of information from Dr. McPherson. He needed to know if there were any other entrances and exits to the hospital other than the general front entrance and the emergency ones.

"I don't want to go snooping around the hospital," he told Roy when he called him very late that evening.

"Mr. Lucky, it's after ten, tell me you found something!" Roy exclaimed.

"Well, I will let you know more in two days' time. I may have a lead, but I need some information, which I am sure you can give me."

"What is it?" Roy said.

There was a little pause at the other end of the line, and then Mr. Lucky started talking again. "Just checking my notes," he said, and then he began with his questioning.

Equipped with all the information he needed, the next day the investigator set out for the security office one last time. The cops did their own inspection of the car, which Rory had brought to the auto shop in Hillcrest. Roy waited to hear from Chief Wells. He needed to have his car repaired; this could take several days or weeks—the thought worried him. He imagined Mr. Lucky solving the puzzle before the cops came up with anything. It was no secret that they dragged their feet too much. However, since Roy did not have any tangible proof to back up his accusation of Grazi's involvement in the tampering of his car, he had to be patient until Mr. Lucky completed his investigation.

Using his usual charm as he entered the security office, Lucky submitted his request and was able to view another tape. This time, it was a surveillance of the front entrance of the hospital. Not wanting to be too much of a nuisance, he decided to concentrate on the hours from three o'clock in the afternoon to five thirty, hoping that he would not have to search further. He was looking for the man in white overalls carrying a toolbox. However, among the many persons entering and leaving the hospital during those hours, no one fitted the description. Lucky refused to be discouraged; his intuition told him that something was not right. He could not request a copy of the tape for further analysis until he had discovered significant data; he just had to keep looking.

Making a careful study of the vehicles as they approached the spot designated for picking up or dropping off patients, he stumbled upon an individual standing with what looked like a piece of white cloth draped over his hand. Lucky became suspicious and decided to examine the location closely. Three cars were parked at the entrance where the man stood; then they each made their way out after picking up their passengers. The last one was a black-and-white minicab. Then after a recorded time of thirty seconds, a car looking very much like the burgundy Mercedes pulled up, and the man got in. There was something in his hand with the white cloth, but it was not clearly visible. The recorded time was three twenty-four.

After obtaining a copy of the tape, the investigator walked over to the garage to take a look at the exit ramp. He remembered that the Mercedes that entered and exited so quickly grazed the steel pole, and he wanted to take a look at it. The ramp had a sharp turn, and over time, few vehicles suffered the same fate. But he knew from experience that the dark-red paint dust he brushed off from the pole was fairly recent. Having collected the dust in a piece of note paper, he set off for his lab. Lucky had a big job ahead of him; he had to find that Mercedes. Maybe the man in the overalls had something to do with the tampering of Roy's car, and the only way to prove that is to find the burgundy Mercedes with license plate ending with a figure four. He knew he could rely on his connections at the Department of Motor Vehicles to facilitate this information, but first he had to make sure he was correct on the year of the model.

When the tape was analyzed, the enlarged objects confirmed his suspicions that the white cloth draped over the man's hand could well be overalls. As he moved to the other side of the car, the object that stuck out from under the cloth proved to be a piece of wood—a toolbox maybe. Lucky's hypothesis was that the man had to be dropped off at the spot where Roy's car was parked to make it less conspicuous than walking around the parking lot in search of it.

This was satisfying news for Roy. He knew he could rely on Mr. Lucky. He was one of the few private investigators in the town of Hillcrest who was not on the take from Jacob Grazi and had a reputation for being exceptionally good in his field. Nevertheless, while the investigation progressed, Roy could not let his guard down. If Grazi tried to put his life in danger before, he would not stop there. The thought was daunting, but he had a lot more to deal with and refused to be distracted. Lucky knew he had to wrap up his investigation quickly in order for charges to be brought about.

Although it was already night when he left the doctor's home, he made a phone call to an associate who helped expedite the information he needed from the Department of Motor Vehicles. The next morning at ten o'clock, a courier arrived at the investigator's office with a package that contained every detail about the Mercedes. It was registered to a notorious businessman who owned a small garbage disposal company in Bayswater, a town just outside of Hillcrest. So without hesitation, Mr. Lucky set out in search of the man.

When he arrived at the place, he parked his car in the middle of the block and walked up the noisy narrow street to an open parking lot, which had two laid-up garbage trucks and a small shabby office building in the far corner. There were mountains of truck tires along the fence and a sign over the entrance, which read "You Trash It, We Remove It." Lucky walked in unnoticed and began to look around casually before entering the office. A young lad sitting behind a pile of rubble called out to him. As he turned to look at the chap, he saw the back of a car that was parked between a brick wall and the fence. Ignoring the lad, he hurried over to take a look at the car, which appeared to be the Mercedes. The young lad rushed to where Lucky stood examining the long scrape on the car.

"Who did this?" he said as he ran his finger along the mark.

"Beats me," said the lad. "But why do you want to know?"

"Oh, just interested in vintage cars," Lucky said. "Could I take a look inside?" He peeped through the tinted windows.

"I have to get the key," the chap muttered as he ran off.

At that moment, the investigator took a small camera from his pocket and started taking pictures of the car and its license plate. He was just about finished when the chap returned, announcing that his uncle would be out as soon as he was off the phone. The investigator did not answer him. Instead, he turned and pretended to walk in the direction of the little office. The lad returned to his spot behind the rubble with headphones pressed into his ears and a tiny radio in his hand. Stepping out of sight, Lucky drifted to another pile of rubble at the side of the shabby building. He was amazed to see two license plates stuck in an old tub next to a small can of black paint and a paintbrush. Just as he bent over to pick them up, he heard a voice behind him saying, "Can I help you?"

"I think you can," Lucky replied as he scooped up the plates and turned around.

A slim-built man stood behind him looking strangely familiar. He appeared to be nervous and kept looking at the license plates in Lucky's hand.

"Who drives the Benz?" Lucky asked.

"Who wants to know?" the man replied.

"Well, I'm interested in the car, can I have a look at it?" Lucky kept staring at the man as he spoke; this made him very uncomfortable.

"It belongs to my boss, and he is not here at the moment. I suggest you come back later." The man then turned and entered the building.

Lucky followed him inside still holding on to the two license plates. "What can you tell me about these?" he asked, turning over the plates to reveal the so-called professional registration.

The man got nervous. "I had nothing to do with that," he blurted out. "It's between my boss and his highfalutin friend. I knew that was a bad idea in the first place."

"What was?" Lucky asked, but the man simply replied that he had nothing more to say and asked the investigator to leave.

"I'll call again," Lucky said as he moved toward the door. "Let me put these back where I found them." He made sure to shut the badly hinged door behind him so he could not be seen as he photographed the license plates where he found them. When he reached the gate, he noticed the young lad stacking tires. "I did not get your uncle's name," he shouted to the lad.

"Flynn!" the lad shouted back.

"As in Errol?" Lucky shouted with laughter.

"No, Sam as in Samuel!" the lad shouted loud enough for Lucky to hear as he hurried down the sidewalk.

It was all coming together, but there was still nothing to implicate Jacob Grazi or even link the Mercedes and the man in the white overalls to the crime. The investigator knew he had to dig deeper still. His intuition told him that Sam Flynn from the garbage company was the weak link, and he had to find a way to make him talk.

With a little research, he found out that the man had a sordid past and was indicted on one occasion several years ago. So he paid him a visit again; this time, he waited for him outside his home. The man became afraid when he saw Lucky. He wanted to ignore him but knew that would be a bad idea, so he complied with his wishes to join him in his car, thinking Lucky to be a fed officer. The investigator handed the man a mock file with papers pertaining to his past run-in with the law and struck a bargain with him in exchange for leniency for his involvement in the garage incident. This was stepping out on a limb, but it all paid off. The man admitted to being the one who cut the brake cables on the doctor's car but said he was threatened by his boss and his friend—the one they call Grazi—into going along with the plan. He explained that he deliberately left the job incomplete so that the fault could be discovered before anyone was seriously hurt and pointed out that he did not accept a penny of the money Grazi paid his boss to get the job done.

This was enough information to bring about charges and stop Grazi in his tracks. He had escaped penalty once before because of lack of sufficient evidence, but this time proved to be different. Lucky made his report complete with photographs, then arranged a meeting with Roy. The overwhelming evidence took him all of ten days to compile.

"How did you do it?" Roy asked after listening to the recording of Sam Flynn's confession.

"Hey! Why do you think they call me Lucky Charm?" The investigator slapped his cheek as he spoke. Then rising out of the chair, he announced, "I have to leave now, I'll send you an invoice later. Let me know if I can be of further assistance."

Roy thanked the man and escorted him to the door.

"You be careful now," Lucky cautioned as he left.

Rory accompanied his brother to another meeting with Chief Wells. This time, they had all the evidence he needed to file charges against Grazi and his friends. When this was done, Roy met with Mrs. Brimm at the hospital and told her what to expect.

"Jake is threading on thin ice here," she said. "I hope our company does not suffer any ill effects for his poor judgment and actions. Now I'll have good reason to remove him from our board of directors. Your father should have done so long ago, but he was too compassionate." She said this to Roy in an outburst of anger.

"I hear Cara will be going home soon." Roy cleverly changed the subject, which made the middle-aged lady composed. "I hear she is making remarkable progress, and I plan to be present when she has her evaluation tomorrow. Will let you know how it goes," he added.

Mrs. Brimm welcomed the change in conversation. "Yes, she can now walk without assistance and looks forward to her homecoming."

Roy felt a deep satisfaction when he heard this. "I hope it won't be too long before I can visit again," he said, but the smile on his face could not hide the concern in his eyes.

After Mrs. Brimm left, he slumped down in his chair, thinking about the demands the upcoming case would have on his time and wondering how he was going to handle whatever publicity may arise from it all.

It was life as usual back at the farm. No one knew, with the exception of Sandy and Rory, about the recent attempts on Roy's life. Fiona had no idea that her sons were aware of their eldest brother's inheritance or that Jacob Grazi was responsible for the attempt to involve him in an accident. She had some concern for Roy's new relationship with the family of Steven Brimm and often confided in Sandy about it. Now her thoughts were occupied with the construction that began on the extension to the Hillcrest Hospital. Her son had made it possible, and she was proud of him and hoped that he would be acknowledged for it. However, her life was taking on a new dimension, one that would throw her right back into the past—a place she thought she had left finally—and she was not aware of it.

Roy had already advised Mrs. Brimm about the impending case against Grazi; now it was time to tell his mother. This knowledge made Fiona nervous and upset. She imagined the type of publicity it may have and hated the idea of being forced to talk about the birth she had protected for so long.

"You don't need to say anything," Roy consoled his mother. "Dad and I will take care of whatever needs to be taken care of."

Chief Wells did a good job of building up a case against Grazi and his accomplices. He made sure to gather enough information to complement the evidence he had received so that all charges would stick. Grazi took the accusation lightly. He felt that he had enough clout to beat the system as he had done before, but he did not count on the confessions of one man whom the police had in protective custody.

The months that followed proved to be long and arduous for both families. In keeping with her decision, Mrs. Brimm removed Grazi from the company's board of directors. She told him it was a temporary arrangement until the trial was over. However, she knew and had hoped it would not be so. She could not tolerate the undignified man with whom bribery was a way of life and did not care for him to be a part of her family enterprise.

The case opened up a whole can of worms for Jacob Grazi. Not only did Sam Flynn confess to his involvement in the car plot, he also linked Grazi to other unsolved heinous crimes, which he and his boss helped cover up. Fiona was relieved that the case took such a twist. There was no question about her son's ancestry or the reason he was being blackmailed. When it was all over, Jacob Grazi and his accomplice each got a five-year prison sentence for their part in conspiring to cause bodily harm, but they faced further indictments on other charges—the penalty for which would keep them behind bars for a lifetime. Sam Flynn was freed because of his testimony and cooperation with the police and was kept in witness protection.

Chapter 14
A Dream Becomes Reality

Both Fiona and Sandy were glad to get back to their daily routine of farm life. However, there were so many questions to be answered where the family was concerned that Fiona felt she could no longer keep silent about the kinship of her eldest son, Roy. She knew it was time to confide in her mother and did so soon after the case was over. Elsie Leighton always had her suspicions about the identity of Roy's father and hoped for the day when her daughter would reconcile with the past, since she herself had long released the resentment she held for the Brimm family. Nevertheless, it was a bit surprising for Fiona that her mother's reaction to the new information was so guarded. Elsie hugged her daughter and thanked her for the wonderful grandson she gave her. Then after kissing her on both cheeks, she whispered gently in her ear, "Let us never speak about this again."

At a family dinner the following weekend, Fiona expressed her readiness to talk about Roy's ancestry since she was aware that her children were anxious over recent events that had impeded their family's serenity. However, before she could do so, Roy admitted that he already had a talk with his brothers after an encounter with Grazi, and they were told about his inheritance.

"What about your sister?" Fiona asked.

"Well, Mom, I'll leave that to you," Roy said casually.

Fiona took a long hard look at her family as they sat around the dinner table, chatting, smiling, teasing one another, and cheering on their dad as he carved the huge side of roast, which he carefully seared on the barbeque pit. Then summoning their silence, she said, "Let's have a toast for the new hospital wing at Hillcrest, which Roy made possible."

For a brief moment, there was silence. All eyes were on Roy.

"Yes, let's hear about this!" Raymond exclaimed in a low voice. Rory frowned at his younger brother, signaling him to shut up, but Rose was curious.

"What is this all about, Roy?" she asked.

"Did you leave some for me?" Ralphie chimed in.

"I said to the new hospital wing!" Fiona shouted over the voices again and raised her glass.

"To the new hospital wing!" everyone repeated.

Roy smiled as he glanced at the quizzical stares around the table. "Quit asking for a corvette, Ralphie, you're not getting one," he teased, and that opened up the discussion about his inheritance. Surprisingly, no one asked about Roy's newfound relatives. They had no idea that the family he had only just acquainted himself with would become such an important part of their lives.

It had been quite a while since Roy visited the Brimm family. The Christmas holidays were fast approaching, and Cara had fully recuperated, having left the hospital several months before. He knew she would be eager to get on with her young adult life. The kind doctor always inquired about the girls from their mother. However, both he and Trudy thought it would be nice to see them again. Roy had no idea when it all began, that feeling of compassion for the children of Steven Brimm. He secretly hated the idea that he was meant to be their guardian angel, but try as he may, he could not escape the urge to concern himself with their well-being. So on a cold Sunday in December, without much coaxing, he and his family accepted an invitation to lunch with the Brimms.

The short drive to the residence was enough to put the little boys to sleep, indicating their nap time had come, although the resounding welcome from two young people who obviously had been starved for a connection with family was enough to startle little Rickey. As the friendship between the couple and the girls grew, the realization that they had no other relatives made it particularly difficult for Roy to ignore their need to belong. Steven Brimm's only brother died at a young age, and Mrs. Brimm was an only child, so there were no cousins on either side. The only other relatives were those of Jacob Grazi and his sister, and they were long estranged from the family. It was a particularly cold and windy afternoon, but the excitement and affectionate laughter of the girls as they played with little Rickey and the baby brought such warmth to the room that it felt like a breath of fresh summer air.

"It really is the first time they have such little ones to play with," their mother said with strange sadness. "You must come more often."

"The girls are also welcome to visit whenever they want to see the children," Trudy announced.

"Oh yes yes yes! I would like that very much," Cara pleaded.

"Me too!" shouted Jane, and everyone burst into laughter when little Rickey added, "Meee too."

Dark winter clouds moved in quickly, casting a shadow over the late afternoon sky in anticipation of the onset of an early evening. The McPhersons said their good-byes and left the Brimm family, hailing good wishes for the coming holiday. It had been a relaxing and enjoyable afternoon for Roy and Trudy but exhausting for the kids who fell fast asleep as soon as the car hit the road. Roy remembered his promise to Cara and was determined to keep it. Although he made no mention of it during their visit, he thought about taking the girl dancing and discussed it with Trudy on their way home.

"She certainly is walking well," he said. "Why don't we take her with us to our usual New Year's Eve party? I'm sure she will be thrilled to know I remembered the promise I made to take her dancing after she had her surgery."

"I think that would be a good way to get her into circulation," Trudy agreed. "But first, you have to get her mother's approval."

"Oh, I have no doubt she will approve," Roy responded wearily. "We still have more than a week at hand. I will think about it, then call her. It should be a good way for Cara to celebrate her new life."

That year, Trudy and the family spent Christmas in Hillcrest with Grandma Leighton. It had been years since all the family gathered there to celebrate Christmas. Elsie Leighton was particularly elated that Gerald and his family could make the trip to be with them since they traveled quite a lot with the orchestra and were hardly ever around on important days. Aunt Violet had been ailing for some time, and the family thought it best that she be placed in a nursing home, seeing that Elsie was too aged to cope with caring for her sister. That was to be the last year their old aunt spent Christmas at home with them. While the realization made it a bit poignant for everyone, it was Aunt Violet's feisty spirit that kept joy in the holiday. Although bedridden, she told lousy stories from her youth and made sure no one entered the bedroom without bringing her a glass of wine. But when full glasses began piling up on the dresser, Aunt Violet simply laughed it off and said she drank much slower than people walked in and out.

Elsie Leighton knew it was a hard task taking care of her sister, but she did not want to be far away from her either. So when Fiona and Sandy suggested that they look into finding a facility near Meadowbrook Farm, Elsie was totally against it. It took some convincing to have her accept the fact that she should consider moving to the farm with them also. That meant giving up the house on Sunny Lane, but Elsie was not sure she felt ready to do so.

The completion of the new hospital wing was extremely gratifying for Dr. McPherson and his family. Everyone was eager to attend the opening ceremony, which honored Roy for his sterling contribution. The dream he had envisioned so long ago had finally become real. However, the unveiling of the bronze plaque above the entrance brought a stare of discontent from Fiona. She wondered why it had been called the Brimm Auditorium when it was all her son's idea to donate his fortune for that cause.

"Pull yourself together, Mother," Roy whispered in her ear when he was able to get close enough to where she stood, obviously distracting herself by having a second look at the program with a scowl on her face.

"Whose suggestion was it?" she asked.

"It was mine, all mine," Roy answered. "The money was his, I did not want it, remember?"

"Who else knew about it?" she asked.

"No one, not even his family. As a matter of fact, I can see Mrs. Brimm making her way toward us. I must introduce you."

"Please don't bother," Fiona pleaded, but before she could move on, Sandy joined them.

"That was an honorable thing to do," he said to his son, his face beaming with admiration. Just then a soft voice interrupted them.

"Hello, Dr. McPherson."

Turning around, Roy noticed the lady. "Hello, Mrs. Brimm. These are my parents, Fiona and Sandy McPherson."

"It is a pleasure to finally meet you," the lady said, and then turning to Roy, she smiled and shook her head. "I must admit I always wanted to know why you were so eager to get rid of your shares in the company. Why didn't you tell me?"

"The hospital needed a new wing more than I needed the shares," he replied.

Then catching Fiona by the hand as she was about to slip away, Mrs. Brimm said, "You have every reason to be proud of him. He is a fine doctor and a perfect gentleman."

Fiona smiled; a soft thank you formed her lips.

"That's our son!" Sandy exclaimed. "He truly is a man of distinction."

Roy patted his father on the back, excused himself, and left the group. Fiona felt a strange awkwardness in the presence of Mrs. Brimm. Seeing her discomfort, Sandy encouraged the ladies to move into the atrium for refreshments. It was there that Fiona let her guard down when they were quickly joined by Trudy, Rose, and Cara. She looked on admiringly as the girls chatted and listened to Cara's outspoken praise for Roy and his encouragement, which helped her have the operation that allowed her to walk properly.

"I'm so glad we got to know him," the young lady said to Fiona. "And I'm happy to meet his wonderful parents and sister at last."

Fiona felt warm inside. Sandy smiled appreciatively when his wife stretched across the table to squeeze Cara's hands with motherly affection.

"Will you allow them to visit?" she asked Mrs. Brimm.

"I'm sure the girls would be thrilled," their mother replied with softness in her voice that signaled the beginning of a strange friendship between the two families.

Since Jacob Grazi was safely behind bars for a very long time, the family was once again quite happy and complacent with their everyday lives as the years went by. Elsie Leighton had been living alone for some time since her sister, Violet, passed away in a nursing home more than a year ago. Fiona was determined to have her mother live with her even if it meant giving up farm life and moving back to the home she grew up in. Rory had taken over full control of the day-to-day running of the farm and factory; he employed more staff to cope with the heavy workload and an accountant to help his father with payroll and other financial matters. It was the age of computers, and that simplified matters very much, but not for Sandy who preferred to stick to his old way of doing things. However, when the question of moving away from the farm came up, Sandy was not too thrilled. Rose and her family lived in a suburban town. Roy and his family lived in Hillcrest. Raymond and Ralphie shared city digs. Rory and his family were the only ones who lived close to the farm. Furthermore, Sandy was not prepared to give up the farmhouse until he was sure that Rory was ready to live there. Although in good condition, the house was very old, and Sandy had signed a petition with the village many years before to preserve the old historical farmhouses. Therefore, modernizing it was not an option.

It didn't seem like any of their younger sons desired to move back to farm life. Raymond had plans to relocate shortly after his forthcoming marriage to take up a new assignment with the bank's head office in Philadelphia while Ralphie had made a bid to purchase the condo where they lived. Therefore, faced with the tough decision of which place would be best for her mother to live, Fiona once again found herself torn between a rock and a hard place. She was sitting in front of the telephone, thinking of the conversation she just had with her mother, when her thoughts were suddenly interrupted by a loud knock on the kitchen door. She opened it to find one of the farmworkers standing with a large basket of fruit and vegetables on his head and several stems of sunflowers in his hand.

"What am I to do with all this produce?" she asked.

Just then, Sandy shouted from the bottom of the stairs, pointing to three similar baskets, "Our donation to the farmers' market at Elsie's church."

Fiona smiled. The farmers' market always raised huge funds for the church; it was something they were committed to doing ever since they started farming. *Yes, this is the most rewarding part of having the farm,* Fiona contemplated. At that moment, she knew she had to give more thought to leaving it.

Accompanied by Sandy, she made the trip to Hillcrest for the farmers' market fund-raising event and reluctantly stopped by to pick up her mother. Fiona preferred if Elsie did not go since it meant having to erect a shade and drag along a comfortable chair, but it was impossible to keep her away as the old lady enjoyed sitting at the fruit stall inviting customers to purchase her produce. Elsie wanted to participate no matter what; she was a hardy old gal who welcomed every opportunity to be outdoors. It mattered not if all she did was sit and look on while Sandy and Fiona set up a stand and arranged the cornucopia of fruit and vegetables to be sold.

Parishioners looked forward to the annual farmers' market and flocked to the site while vendors were still setting up their stalls, walking around in circles surveying all the baskets in an effort to get the best picks for themselves. It didn't take long for Sandy and Fiona to sell out all they had brought, including the giant sunflowers, which went quickly at two dollars apiece.

"Maybe next year, we get to be customers instead of vendors," Fiona whispered to her mother.

"What do you mean?" Elsie asked.

Her questioning glance made Fiona smile sheepishly. "If we move in with you, we will have to give up the farm," she said bluntly, then turned away to help Sandy dismantle the stall and shade. Even though their intention was to turn the farm over to Rory, Fiona did not want her mother to know that. She desperately wanted her willing consent to live there with them.

Elsie was not her usual talkative self on the way home. She knew she had to make a choice, and it had to be one that didn't force her daughter and son-in-law to give up their farm. A cheery voice greeted them as the car pulled up to the house on Sunny Lane. Etta Bentley had dropped in to check on the old lady as she usually did on her way to the library but was concerned when no one answered the door. She was just about to call on a neighbor when Elsie arrived home. The woman's eyes lit up when she saw the old lady being helped out of the car.

"I was worried when you did not answer the door," she said.

"This is my daughter," Elsie told her.

Etta followed as Fiona helped her mother into the house.

"I'm glad she was with you," the woman said.

Fiona's gaze met her mother's.

"That was a sizeable sum we donated. I would hate not being able to do that again next year," Elsie said softly.

"Well, Mother, the choice is yours. Get some rest, and I will fix lunch." Fiona felt satisfied as she left her mother comfortably seated on the sofa and entered the kitchen.

It was early afternoon, and Elsie retired for her usual after-lunch nap, leaving Fiona and Sandy to secure the house when they left.

"Let's make a quick stop to see Trudy and the children," Fiona said cheerily as she entered the car.

Sandy grunted. It had been a long day, and he was tired. Nevertheless, he made the detour to Beaver Place.

"I was expecting you," Trudy said as she opened the door, looking larger than life in her second trimester. "I was over at Grandma Elsie's yesterday, and she told me about the farmers' market. How did you do?"

"Oh, we were sold out within two hours!" Fiona exclaimed, holding out a small bag of fruit. "These are for you."

Trudy took the bag and shouted from the bottom of the stairs, "Pop-Pop and Nana Fi are here, boys!"

A rumbling sound like thunder came from the second floor. Then what sounded like horses hooves on the stairs turned out to be the trampling of Rickey and Graham as they raced to meet their grandparents. Running with outstretched hands and a broad luminescent smile, his curly brown hair tousled as he shook his head from side to side, Graham leaped straight into his grandfather's arms. Rickey approached his grandmother with a speed that could have knocked her off her feet had she not held on to him as he hugged her tightly. What a cheerful welcome from a pair of young boys who were thrilled to see their grandparents.

"Will you wait for Roy and have dinner with us?" Trudy asked.

"Not this time." Sandy chuckled. "We have to get on the road before nightfall. It's been a long day, and the traffic will slow us down some."

Trudy agreed, and after a brief visit, the children waved good-bye to their grandparents.

The ride home was smooth. Fiona let her thoughts wander about the move she was about to have her mother make. Was it unkind to take the old lady away from the independent life she had been living for so long? On the other hand, did she want to move back to Hillcrest? She was not going to leave Sandy alone on the farm and have a visiting relationship. Also, she was not prepared to force him to give up farming before he was ready to. As she contemplated on these things, she glanced at her husband—his weathered hands fastened to the steering wheel, his craggy cheeks altered his ruggedly handsome features. Still Fiona was amazed by the rousing charisma of this husband she found the courage to love so very long ago.

Chapter 15
A New Life Replaces the Old

It was Sunday morning. Roy had an early cup of coffee and went back to bed with the newspapers when the phone interrupted his reading. The headline MOTHER OF HOSPITAL BENEFACTOR MISTREATED BY HOME AIDE" caught his eye. He folded the page and reached for the phone. It was Raymond.

Roy was surprised. "Why such an early call, you need a doctor?"

The two chuckled on the phone. "Man, I'm on my way to the airport. I'll be gone for three days to attend a business meeting and just remembered I didn't tell anyone. Anyway, I'll call Mom from the airport."

"Where are you off to?" Roy asked.

"LA," replied his younger brother. "I called because I just saw an article in the *Sunday Express* that might be of interest to you."

Roy yawned and stretched his legs. "Yes, I was just about to read it when the phone rang," he replied.

"Well, I'll let you get to it. I'll call you when I get back on Wednesday evening."

Roy hung up the phone and continued reading the article that outlined Lonize Brimm as the elderly victim of a cruel home-care worker. Roy wondered about the old lady. He had no idea she was still alive. He wanted to find out more and thought of calling Mrs. Brimm but decided to call his mother instead.

After breakfast, he settled back in his recliner and dialed his mother. She confirmed that Lonize was Steven Brimm's mother but was somewhat surprised that Mrs. Brimm never mentioned her mother-in-law to Roy.

"Are you going to get involved?" Fiona asked.

"No, just curious," Roy replied.

It was already the middle of the workweek when the doctor ran into Mrs. Brimm on the geriatric ward of the new hospital wing. Apparently, she was visiting her mother-in-law when she heard a page for him and rushed out to the nurses' station where she stood, pretending to scrutinize a notice board. When the doctor appeared, he had a quick exchange of greetings with Mrs. Brimm, then took the folder that the head nurse handed him, and turned away while thumbing through the pages.

Mrs. Brimm followed him and tugged at his sleeve. "I was hoping to see you here," she said. "Your grandmother is on this floor. I don't suppose you know about it, but I was hoping you could call on her. She would like to know you, her doctor is Dr. Casey." Mrs. Brimm spoke quickly.

Roy paused. "I read something about it and meant to phone you but have not yet gotten around to doing so. When was she admitted?"

"Yesterday," Mrs. Brimm continued, following the doctor while talking as fast as she could. "I don't want to hold you up, but if you can spare a moment, I will take you to her. My husband told her about you."

Roy stopped, looked at his watch, then squeezed her shoulder. "I have to be at a meeting at 2:45 p.m. I only have ten minutes to spare, can this be done later?"

"Very well then." Mrs. Brimm's disappointment was obvious. "It would only take a minute," she pleaded.

"Then let's make it a quick one," Roy said as he beckoned her to lead the way.

They hurried to a room just down the hall. Bed number 2 was on the scenic side, and the sun shone brightly through the large window pane in the semiprivate room. Crisp white bedding and pastel vertical shades blended with a view of the garden that helped camouflage the sight of commodes and walkers. The frail curled-up figure of a life-size doll turned out to be that of Lonize Brimm.

"Mother." Her daughter-in-law paused for acknowledgment. "Mother, Dr. Rhoyan McPherson is here to see you."

The old lady turned on her back and painfully eased herself into the reclined position she was meant to be in. She looked up at Roy; he bent over and held her hand. A strange familiar feeling overcame him. The overly thin features and sagging cheeks could not disguise a face he knew he had seen once before. Thick eyebrows, which were once brown, seemed bushy in their gray form. Piercing brown eyes appeared blotchy and softened with age. Yes, this was the face of a very angry lady he and his brother encountered as youths while playing on the sidewalk on Sunny Lane.

Roy smiled at the old lady. "Are they taking good care of you?" he asked.

She nodded gently, then caught the end of Roy's tie, and gave it a slight tug.

"She wants you to move closer," her daughter-in-law said. "She can't see your face very well."

Roy bent over a little farther. The old lady lifted her hand and touched his head. She felt his ear, then let her hand slide down to rest on the side of his waist, the same side on which he had the scar. Roy smiled, and her eyes filled with tears.

"I must be going now, but I will check on you again," he told her softly as he eased the grip she had on him.

"Thanks for coming," Mrs. Brimm said to Roy while escorting him to the door. "I will keep you informed of her progress."

"Never mind," the doctor replied quickly. "I will check with Dr. Casey, but I will call you to hear more about the newspaper article." Roy hurried down the hall, and Mrs. Brimm retreated to the bedside of her aged mother-in-law.

"He is a handsome guy and a fine doctor. I'm grateful Steven got to know him," she chatted as she fixed the shades. "He has two sons, and they are expecting a baby any day now." She continued while admiring the view of the garden.

There was a peaceful silence. Mrs. Brimm sighed and then turned to look at her mother-in-law. The old lady lay motionless, her glazed eyes transfixed to the ceiling. A river of tears flowed down her wrinkled cheeks, but an occasional blink gave some assurance that she was still there.

The next day, Roy dropped in to see Lonize Brimm while he was on the floor. Dr. Casey and two of his interns, along with two nurses, were at her bedside. Cara and Jane waited outside the door.

"We don't know what's going on," Jane said when Roy arrived. Her voice trembled as she spoke.

"Well, let's see," he said, walking past them to enter the room.

Dr. Casey had just concluded his examination. One of the nurses took the chart from him and hung it at the foot of the bed while the screen opened up, and Dr. McPherson made his appearance. The doctor washed his hands at the sink and proceeded to the door.

"Dr. Casey, I need to talk to you concerning the old lady," Roy said quietly. "Can we step outside?"

Roy left the room in the company of the middle-aged doctor and his two young interns. Cara and Jane waited for the nurses, who were fixing their grandmother, to leave; then they pulled up chairs by the bedside.

"Have you come to take me home?" the old lady said feebly.

Cara smiled and pulled her chin.

"Do you want to go back home now?" Jane said, knitting her brows.

"Don't be so silly," Cara scolded her sister. "Grams is here to get well, and she knows that."

Just then, Roy came into the room.

"Dr. McPherson! I thought you were not going to come back," Jane said.

"I was just having a talk with Dr. Casey. Your grandmother is in good hands."

The old lady turned her head in Roy's direction when she heard his voice.

"I can see you have a lot of company," he said to her. "I will check back with you later."

She held out her hand, and Roy squeezed it affectionately. Then he patted the back of her hand as he placed it beside her. "Make sure she gets some rest," he said to Jane, then turned and left the room.

Roy looked in briefly on Lonize Brimm every day after that. Despite the good care and treatment of her doctor and the hospital staff, her health slowly declined. On Friday evening, before he left for the weekend, Roy visited the old lady. She seemed to be asleep when he arrived at her bedside, so he stood quietly looking down at her. She must have felt his presence for she opened her eyes after a short while and tried to lift her hand. Roy touched her shoulder. Her lips moved gradually trying to form words. Roy quietly stood there, still watching her and marveled that fate had made their paths cross again in a different way. The effort seemed too much for the old lady; she could not utter the words she so wanted to say. She lifted her glassy eyes and looked at Roy. All at once, the words came to him.

"I know you are happy to see me, I'm glad to know you too." He bent over and kissed her gently on the forehead. "Try to get some rest. I'll see you when I get back to hospital."

Roy straightened up and moved to the window. He closed the shades, then pulled up the bed rails. Her eyes followed him around the room. She smiled faintly as he tucked her in and fixed her pillows. Then as he was about to leave, he touched her shoulder again. "Good-bye, Grandma," he said. She nodded in acknowledgment and turned her head as he slowly walked away.

"Better wake my mother," Trudy said as she sat up in bed very early on Saturday morning. "She will stay with the kids while we go to hospital."

"Hospital?" Roy asked sleepily. "Who's going to hospital?" He was not fully awake.

Trudy was silent. *Maybe I can wait a bit longer,* she thought. So she eased herself out of bed and headed for the bathroom.

As if something had suddenly hit him, Roy jumped up. "Is everything all right?" he called out hoarsely.

"It's time," Trudy announced.

"I hope I have time to get dressed," Roy teased. He got out of bed, rubbing his eyes and yawning widely as he stretched until his bones cracked. "And now for the final round!" he joked.

Trudy sighed heavily.

"I'll call Dr. Bayner and tell him to expect us." His tone was more serious. "Is your mother awake?" he asked.

"I don't know, I'll check on her before we leave."

Roy did not expect to be back at the hospital so early in the weekend. While the nurses looked after Trudy, he slipped into the cafeteria to grab a cup of coffee. It all went so fast. He was lucky to get back to the delivery room in time to witness the birth of his first daughter at 6:57 a.m. The first thing he did when Dr. Bayner placed the baby in his arms was to examine her hips. Trudy looked on as he scrutinized her little body, and his eyes told her that behind his masked face was a beaming smile. She had no scars.

It was midmorning when Roy returned home to the excitement of his two sons. Fiona and Sandy arrived shortly after and offered to take Trudy's mom along with the children to see their new sister. Roy welcomed the idea, which afforded him a few hours of much needed sleep before returning to the hospital. Savoring the peace and quiet, he settled back and quickly fell into a deep slumber only to be awakened by the constant ringing of the doorbell. Looking at his watch, he realized he had been asleep for several hours. The kids had returned home with their grandparents after visiting their mother and stopping by to tell Grandma Elsie about their new sister.

Fiona helped Trudy's mom settle the children and prepare dinner before she and Sandy returned home while Roy hurried off to the hospital to be with his wife. He was in the elevator on his way to the maternity floor when he ran into Dr. Casey and was told about the passing of Lonize Brimm that morning.

"You seemed very interested in her case, Dr. McPherson. Was she a relative?" Dr. Casey asked just before the doors opened up.

"Yes, kind of," Roy replied before he stepped off the elevator.

Congratulatory greetings followed him down the hallway to Trudy's room. He had a perplexed look on his face. Roy hugged his wife and sat in a chair next to the bed, watching her nurse the baby.

"Are you ready to come home tomorrow?" he asked.

"Yes," she replied. "Dr. Bayner said I'm fine. Did you speak to him?"

"I'll call him later," he assured her. Roy chatted with his wife for quite a while but did not mention the passing of Lonize Brimm.

Trudy was tired. She had been having visitors all day and needed to rest, so Roy arranged for the nursery to care for the baby during the night before he left the hospital.

The children were already in bed by the time he arrived home. He ate a satisfying dinner; it was the first good meal he had for the day.

"I think there are a couple of messages on the phone," his mother-in-law announced.

"Thanks, I didn't remember to check."

He knew there would be many congratulatory calls from family and friends, so he got to the messages as soon as he finished dinner. The very first one was from Mrs. Brimm in which she requested a return call. Ignoring the time, Roy returned the call and apologized for calling so late.

"Did you know we lost the old lady?" Mrs. Brimm said.

"Yes," he replied. "My sympathy to you and the family. I ran into Dr. Casey this afternoon, and he mentioned it."

"Did he say why she went so quickly?" Mrs. Brimm asked.

"I only saw him briefly in the elevator and did not have a chance to discuss it at all," Roy explained.

"Were you there?" he asked.

"Yes. By the time I got there, it was all over, so I returned home. I'm sorry, I did not know you were at the hospital today. I should have asked for you, very silly of me." She seemed a bit frustrated with herself as she spoke.

"I was not on call today, but my wife delivered very early this morning," Roy told her.

"Oh yes? What did she have?" Her tone sounded much brighter.

"We are the proud parents of a daughter, seven pounds two ounces," he calmly announced.

"Congratulations! When was she born?" Mrs. Brimm asked cheerily.

"At six fifty-seven this morning," he replied.

"When?" she asked again.

"Six fifty-seven this morning," he repeated. Then there was silence, so Roy continued talking. "So you see, I have been preoccupied most of the day."

He paused for some acknowledgment that she was still listening, but there was none.

"Do you know when the funeral will be?" he asked gently and waited for the reply.

"Yes . . . ah . . . oh sorry, I wanted to let you know that—" Mrs. Brimm quickly snapped out of her trance. "It's just something you said. The funeral will be on Monday morning at the old All Saints Church on the edge of town," she added quickly. "It will be at nine o'clock."

"OK," Roy answered. "I'd like to come if that's all right with you."

"Yes, by all means. She would love you to be there. Also, the girls would appreciate it very much. They were looking forward to visiting her again today but never even got the chance. It all happened so quickly."

"When did she die?" Roy asked.

"At six fifty-seven this morning," she said somberly.

"What a coincidence. Are you sure of the time?" Roy inquired.

"Yes, it was written by the doctor on call."

The conversation left Roy with a weird feeling. His grandmother whom he just got to know was leaving the world while his daughter was being born. Roy wondered what his mother would think of it. The reality was astounding. He quietly listened to the other messages and tried to occupy his mind with the homecoming of his wife and baby. Remembering that he had not yet spoken to Dr. Bayner, he picked up the phone again and was relieved to hear that Trudy could come home the next day.

"You may wish to let the pediatrician on call check the baby before she leaves," Dr. Bayner advised.

"Sure thing!" Roy remarked, then thanked his colleague for taking good care of his wife.

Roy had a restless sleep that night. He tossed and turned unusually, and before he knew it, Sunday morning had arrived. He got up quite early, got the newspapers, and went back to bed, hoping he would feel sleepy again at some point before the kids were awake. As he settled back and opened the paper, his eyes fell on the headline MOTHER OF HOSPITAL BENEFACTOR DIES IN HOSPITAL. He stared at the article, fighting the urge to ignore it, but succumbed to better judgment.

What started out as assault charges for the home aide involved in the mistreatment of the old lady had now turned into a charge of manslaughter. Investigations were still ongoing according to the news report, although Mrs. Brimm failed to mention any of it to Roy. At that point, he wondered if he was being insensitive by not inquiring about the article. He already knew from Dr. Casey that the old lady suffered a heart attack when she was doused with cold water. Was it an accident? Who knew? Did her daughter-in-law have anything to do with instigating the charges? These were all questions that captured his interest. Nevertheless, knowing he would find out the full story soon enough, he dropped the paper and dozed off.

The sound of a small voice calling him together with a tug on his ear made Roy open his sleepy eyes.

"Aren't you going to get Mom?" Graham asked sadly.

"What time is it?" his father asked as he tried to focus on the clock radio that sat on the night table next to him. "Thanks for waking me, son. Did you eat breakfast?"

"Yeah."

"Then tell Mamma I'll be down in a little while."

Roy pulled himself out of bed. Two hours of sleep went a long way toward revitalizing him. He rushed to the bathroom and got himself ready in record time.

"I won't have much to eat," he called out to his mother-in-law who looked surprised when he appeared in the kitchen clean-shaven and well dressed, emitting a mild aroma of posh aftershave.

"You should have a proper breakfast," she scolded.

Roy smiled and sat at the table. He ate as quickly as he could possibly chew, then gulped his coffee, and left for the hospital.

Although they had done it twice before, the homecoming of this baby was different for the couple. There was no longer any uncertainty about family ties, and they were relieved that their daughter bore no conspicuous birthmarks. She was a perfect little girl for which they were both grateful. The couple chatted blissfully on the way home. Trudy was grateful to have her mother take care of the household in her absence and hoped she could stay a little while longer. Although she seemed fine, Roy still noticed a bit of tiredness in his wife's face and ordered her to bed as soon as they arrived home. He had not told her about the old lady or the funeral he had to attend the next morning. They were happy to be home with the new baby to the sheer excitement of their two sons, and nothing else seemed important. The family relaxed and enjoyed what was left of the weekend. Trudy obeyed doctor's orders and stayed in bed most of the day, surfacing only to have a quiet dinner with the family.

On Monday morning, Roy kissed his wife and left home at the crack of dawn. He completed his early rounds at the hospital, then left to attend the funeral of Lonize Brimm, his grandmother. The quaint little church was packed when he arrived. Jane met him at the door and escorted him to a seat they had reserved right where the family sat. The service was simple but touching, and Roy could not help but wonder about the life of this woman who gave birth to his father.

When it was all over, he tried to slip unnoticed through the crowded narrow doorway of the little church to get back to the hospital. He made it all the way out, got into his car, and was about to drive off when he noticed Jane approaching the car with a bunch of flowers in her hand.

"Aren't you coming to the cemetery?" she called out.

"Sorry, Jane, I have to be back at the hospital. I'll see you later."

"You'll be at the reception then, won't you?" she pleaded, forcing herself through the car window to give him a hug. "We will be expecting you!" she exclaimed as she released the grip she had on his neck.

"Please give my apologies to your mom. I have lots to take care of today, but I will call her." With that said, he turned the car around and sped away in the opposite direction.

A few days after, Mrs. Brimm called Roy to thank him for attending the funeral.

"Sorry you could not make it to the reception," she said. "I hope Trudy and the baby are fine."

"Oh yes. We all could do with a bit more sleep, but everyone's fine."

"I would like you to meet me and my attorneys in a few days," she continued. "Just let me know what day is convenient for you, and I will make the appointment."

"What is this all about?" An echo of concern sounded in Roy's voice. "Is it about the investigation?" he inquired.

"What investigation? Oh! No, not at all. I have nothing to do with that, it's all in the hands of the authorities." Mrs. Brimm seemed surprised at the question. "It concerns the reading of the old lady's will," she said bluntly. "I would like to expedite that matter so we can settle her affairs."

Roy was puzzled; he could not believe what he had heard and wondered what Lonize Brimm's will had to do with him. Not wanting to appear pessimistic in any way, he responded carefully. The thought of another inheritance troubled him. That was not the kind of news he cared to hear about.

"Do you really need me to be in attendance?" he asked. The seriousness of his voice displayed his concern.

"I would greatly appreciate it if you could be there," the good lady said. "There's nothing to worry about. Just let me know soon what day is suitable for you."

"Well then, I'll call you in a couple of days," he spoke graciously, and Mrs. Brimm was satisfied.

"I hope we will get a chance to see the newborn in the coming months," she said.

"Certainly," Roy responded, and after some casual conversation, he excused himself to have dinner.

The phone call left him with an uncertain feeling, one of déjà vu, and he sighed heavily as he responded to Trudy's repeated call for dinner. Roy sat at the table with his chin buried in his chest and eyes closed as if in prayer. His wife pretended not to notice, but the waning of his appetite aroused some concern.

"What's up with you? Is it the phone call?"

"Nah, I'm just not that hungry," he said, then got up, and removed his plate. "I'll save this for later, maybe I'll have it before going to bed."

Trudy frowned and shook her head. She knew there was something bothering him but decided to leave it for the time being. She did not know about Lonize Brimm's passing at the time she was giving birth or that her husband attended the funeral the day after she came home with her new baby. Roy needed some time to think before discussing the possibility of another inheritance. He also wanted to find out what the importance of his presence was at the reading of the will. So after much contemplation, he decided to let Mrs. Brimm know that he was available to meet with her attorneys the following day.

The afternoon was bright and sunny when he pulled into a parking space right next to where Mrs. Brimm was parked. He was met in the lobby by a chubby short young lady with a cheerful personality and was escorted to a room where the elderly lady sat with her attorney and two of his partners.

"So glad you could spare the time, Doctor!" the man remarked. "We won't keep you long, just a few formalities. You may sit wherever you feel comfortable, and we can begin."

Mrs. Brimm nodded to Roy, and he sat next to her. The man wasted no time in opening a folder, which revealed the documents. Roy sat motionless with a solemn face as the words that bequeathed him with the house and property of the Brimm estate leaped off the pages and connected to his ears. He could not understand what he was hearing. It made no sense at all. Mrs. Brimm simply glanced at him and smiled as if to assure him that he had nothing to worry about. When it was all over, the three gentlemen in the room congratulated Roy and proceeded with the signing of documents for transfer of the property. Roy looked at the papers that were placed before him, pushed them aside, and turned to Mrs. Brimm.

"Can I have a quick word with you in private?" he whispered, then got up, and left the room. The elderly lady followed close behind. "I'm sorry," he said.

But before he could continue, Mrs. Brimm interrupted. "I know what you are going to say, but first hear me out." She beckoned him to sit beside her in a small alcove beside a water cooler. Then taking a medium-sized notebook out of her handbag, she told him why he had inherited the property.

"Your father's great-grandfather came to this country as an infant with his mother, who hid him in a ship bound for America to spare his life since he was deformed and her family felt he should be put away. The two lived in humble dwellings, and the child's mother died when he was twelve years old. Having no means of support, he hired himself out as a water boy at construction sites. He collected stray nails and screws and traded them for food and crawled under tarpaulins to sleep at night. To keep himself occupied, he gathered small bits of wood from under the carpenters' workbench in which he carved designs with a pocket knife. When that lad was sixteen years old, he was apprenticed to an elderly carpenter who taught him the art of building. When he grew up, he married the man's daughter and fathered two children. His daughter died as an infant, but his son who was terribly scarred survived his childhood, and so his father made sure he was educated.

"When the boy finished school, he worked for a builder and learned all he could about the trade. His job brought him to Hillcrest where he met a young woman and married her after a short courtship. They had nowhere to live, so he brought his widowed father to help him build a small house on a plot of land he paid for with his wages. The two struggled for one year building the house while living on the site. They could not afford to employ more hands. The young man helped his father when his job allowed him some free time. When the house was finally completed, the old man presented the young couple with some furniture he made and resided with them for the rest of his life. Before he died, he made his son promise that he would never sell or trade his home. It must be passed on to sons of future generations, and that line stops with you." Mrs. Brimm paused long enough for it all to sink in; then she continued, "You see, Doctor, your father inherited this house from his father who enlarged it, and your father also had a few renovations done."

"Surely there were others?" Roy asked.

"Yes, your father's grandfather had two daughters and one son. One daughter died as a child, and the other was married to Vincent Grazi. She had Jacob and his sister. His son, who was scarred like his father, had two sons: your father and your uncle who died as a young man." Handing the book to Roy, she said, "It's all in here, you may read it for yourself. It's yours now. It is quite fitting that you and your sons should inherit the property as the Brimm bloodline leads to you. Your name may be McPherson, but the name of that deformed baby who beat all the odds and survived a perilous sea voyage was Rhoyan Brimm. Your grandmother was very comforted that your mother named you Rhoyan."

Roy was overcome with emotion. He took the book and thumbed through the pages. Untidy large handwriting that signaled the work of an elderly person covered every page.

"I will go back in now," Mrs. Brimm said and walked away, leaving Roy to himself.

He sat for a while staring at the notebook, then leaped up, and went back to the room. Taking his place next to Mrs. Brimm again, he read and signed all the papers. The house and vintage Chevy was left to Roy. Furniture and furnishings were to be auctioned off and the money given to Lonize Brimm's favorite charities.

Roy took the notebook home and gave it to his wife to read. He told her about the passing of Lonize Brimm and about the new inheritance.

Trudy laughed nervously. "Are you sure this is fine with you? I knew something was bothering you. Where does it all end?" she asked cautiously.

"Apparently, it ends here with me," he said abruptly. "So I'll do what I have to, I suppose." Roy shrugged his shoulders as he spoke.

"What about your parents?" she asked.

"What about them?" he returned.

"Well, are you going to tell them about this matter?"

"Of course, I need them to know. Mom will be coming soon to help Grandma with her packing, and I will ask them to stop by."

In the days that followed, Roy visited the property with Mrs. Brimm to take possession of the keys and acquaint himself with the place his ancestors built. He encouraged her to keep all the furniture that was made by the family and have it exhibited in a special room at the company's headquarters. Mrs. Brimm was delighted with the idea and arranged for the Brimm craftsmanship to be removed from the house before the auctioneers arrived.

When Fiona and Sandy heard about their son's new inheritance, they were both a bit concerned and questioned the legality of it. However, Roy made sure they read the family's notebook, which helped to dispel some of their concerns.

"What will you do with the house?" his mother asked.

"I'm not sure. I will wait until the auction is over and it is cleared of all the furnishings, then I will decide. There is also the vintage Chevy. I heard it's in working condition, but I haven't looked at it yet." Roy rubbed his forehead as he spoke.

Sandy and Fiona exchanged glances, but nothing more was said. She had a strange feeling about the life she had given birth to and had fiercely protected from the family she loathed for so long. But destiny had a way of changing things, and Fiona had already come to grips with the reality of the strange fate that brought them back to a place and time that will forever be etched in her life and the life of her firstborn.

The day had finally arrived for Elsie to move to the farm. Sandy and Fiona had made the final trip to collect her. All her personal belongings had already been moved to their home in Meadowbrook, and the old lady was quite contented with the arrangement. The family had planned on spending a few weekends every year in Hillcrest as well as some of the Christmas and Thanksgiving holidays, so the house was left intact with all the furniture and furnishings. Fiona took several white cotton sheets to cover the upholstery after the house was cleaned and prepared. Saturdays were always very quiet in the neighborhood; and Elsie sat on her bed, enjoying the chirping of the birds outside her window, while Sandy helped Fiona spread sheets on tables and chairs. Roy had called to say he would stop by to see his grandmother before they left. He had visited the Brimm family home after the auctioneers had left and was going to take the old car for a test run on his way over. However, when his parents were ready to leave, he had not arrived. Sandy packed the car with the rest of Elsie's belongings—a suitcase, her walker, and a few hat boxes—then helped his mother-in-law into the backseat while they waited for Fiona.

It was a bright and sunny summer day. Fiona stood at the window of that weather-worn two-storied Victorian house; her eyes focused down Sunny Lane, hoping to see her son as he drove along in the old Chevy. When he approached, her eyes filled with tears as she remembered how eager she was to look at that same Chevy as it sped down the road when she was young. Wiping away her tears, she quickly stepped outside and locked the door, making her way to the gate to greet her son.

10/16 NS

CPSIA information can be obtained at www.ICGtesting.com
Printed in the USA
BVOW01s1100141013

333688BV00001B/16/P

9 781465 385697